Growing Up
BRONX

A NOVEL BY
Gerald Rosen

NORTH ATLANTIC BOOKS, BERKELEY, CALIFORNIA

Growing Up Bronx
Copyright © 1984 by Gerald Rosen

ISBN 0-938190-36-9 (pbk.)
ISBN 0-938190-37-7 (cloth)

Publisher's Address: North Atlantic Books
                     2320 Blake Street
                     Berkeley, California 94704

Cover Art by Jaqui Gunto
Cover and Book Design by Paula Morrison
Typeset in Baskerville by Birthe Rasmussen and Stan Shoptaugh

Growing Up Bronx is sponsored by the Society for the Study of Native Arts and Sciences, a nonprofit educational corporation whose goals are to develop an ecological and crosscultural perspective linking various scientific, social, and artistic fields; to nurture a holistic view of arts, sciences, humanities, and healing; and to publish and distribute literature on the relationship of mind, body, and nature.

Library of Congress Cataloging in Publication Data
Rosen, Gerald.
     Growing up Bronx.

     I. Title.
PS3568.765G7   1984   813'.54   84-1193
ISBN 0-938190-37-7
ISBN 0-938190-36-9 (pbk.)

For Marijke

This book is a novel, a work of fiction.
None of the characters should be confused
with anyone living or dead.

Anon I rose
As if on wings and saw beneath me stretched
Vast prospect of the world which I had been
And was; and hence this Song . . .

William Wordsworth

Chapter 1

I was born on January 6, 1939.

The place into which I was born has been called by many names:
The Jewish people call it the Diaspora, the land of exile and aliena-
tion. The Hindus call it maya, the veil of illusion. The Christians call
it a vale of tears or a testing ground for the human soul. The Buddhists
call it samsara, the ocean of birth and death.

I call it The Bronx.

I was born in the Royal Hospital on the Grand Concourse. The
name they gave me was Danny. Danny Schwartz.

The beginning of 1939 was not an especially auspicious time for
a Jewish child to be born into the world, but I was not to begin to
realize this until I was much older. Until I was five. At that time I
found out that, in Europe, there was a man with a mustache who
wanted to kill everyone in our neighborhood. I was just a boy, not
wise in the ways of the world, but somehow this did not seem reasonable
to me.

The fact that my father, Sid Schwartz, also had a mustache further
confused matters.

My personal circumstances at birth were not unfavorable. My
grandfather, Ben Farber, my mother's father, born in Austria, had
started as a baker and had invested in real estate in The Bronx just
when the Jews began to move there from Harlem and the Lower East
Side of Manhattan. The Bronx was the third stop on the Jewish Oregon
Trail which continued on to a fourth stop in Yonkers and Mt. Vernon.

The fifth and final stop on this trail was Jewish nirvana, also known as the Greater Miami area.

By the beginning of the Second World War my grandfather had retired from baking. He owned two large apartment houses including the one my parents lived in, and he had helped several other bakers to get away from the oven by guiding them in real estate investments and loaning them money. He never learned to read or write English.

My grandmother, Yettie Farber, my mother's mother, was also from Austria. She was a very nice woman but I feel she did not serve to give me the most positive self-image when I was a child. Her name for me, when she was angry at me, was "*schmutz.*" She used to shout at me, "Dee *schmutz,* dee!" *Schmutz* in Yiddish means dirt.

To be fair, I must admit that, as grandson of the landlord and an incipient Jewish prince, there were times when I merited a worse epithet than the relatively innocuous "*schmutz.*"

In fact, my grandmother was a gentle, homebound, generous woman, dedicated to the hearth and family, modest and generally taciturn except for those instances when she would wail and scuttle back and forth across the room like a wounded bear in a penny- arcade shooting-gallery machine. She would do this whenever my grandfather would try to hit my Uncle Bernie.

Bernie was my mother's older brother, a flashy dresser who drove a big car, drank, told one-line jokes, played the piano using only the black keys, and felt he should have been in Hollywood. When he drove his Packard to the East Bronx record store in which he worked, he always wore a carnation in his lapel. He paid a black man named Grover to park his car for him and to call him "Money." Whenever Grover called Bernie "Money," Bernie gave him a big tip. Like his two sisters—my mother, Ceil Schwartz, and my mother's younger sister, Rose—he was a big tipper.

My father wasn't a big tipper, but he did believe in leaving a fair tip, especially when a waiter let him move to the front of a line in a restaurant or when he took me to the one basketball game we ever went to together and the ticket taker at Yankee Stadium let me crawl under the turnstile without a ticket.

My father's family, the Schwartzes, were of a lower socio-economic class than my mother's family, the Farbers. He grew up on the Lower East Side with his younger sisters, Fanny and Hilda, and his four older brothers whom we didn't see that often because they lived far away from us on the other side of the world.

They lived in Brooklyn.

When I was growing up we lived next door to my mother's parents and my Aunt Rose who lived with them. We lived over a restaurant, Blum's, which was situated in the ground floor walk-in apartment of the building my grandfather owned on Nelson Avenue. My Uncle Bernie used to kid us about living over a restaurant but, as my Aunt Rose used to say, it was better than living *under* a restaurant.

My Uncle Bernie and my Aunt Bessie lived two blocks away in the grandest building in our part of The Bronx—the Noonan Plaza. At the center of the building's courtyard, which was landscaped with gardens, was a large cement pond spanned by a bridge. In the pond resided two live swans.

There were no swans where my father grew up. His parents had come over from Russia a few years before he was born. My father had skipped a year in school and would have graduated from high school at the age of sixteen, but at thirteen he had to leave school to earn money sweeping movie theaters because his father died.

As a result of his early experience my father knew the value of a dollar. He knew that a working person had to make a living and should get an adequate tip if the occasion called for it. In fact, sometimes he would go downstairs to Blum's where his sister Fanny worked as a waitress and if, while he was talking to her, a customer left without tipping her, my father would say in a loud, angry voice, "Did he stiff you, Fanny? Fanny, tell me the truth. Did that son of a bitch stiff you?"

Fanny didn't tell him the truth since that time when she did reveal to him that a man hadn't tipped her and my father chased the man up the street accusing him of "stiffing my sister" until they got into a fight and the man broke my father's glasses.

Besides rimless glasses and a thin mustache my father also wore a shadowed, hungry look. He was five foot nine and wiry with leathery skin that seemed to fit his face too tightly, like new shoes, giving him an intense and pain-filled expression. He had dark, thin, oily hair and several visible gold teeth. He wore bow ties and smoked two or three packs of Chesterfields a day, always forgetting to flick the ashes off his cigarette until they grew too long and toppled onto his shirt.

When I was a small child I liked to point to the ash as it was about to fall. He would flick it off and notice me and be grateful to me.

My mother was an attractive woman who felt she should have been "discovered" by somebody. She had studied tap dancing and "modern" dance and was pretty enough to have had her picture in the paper several times when she was younger. She did dance professionally for a brief time in a night club in Philadelphia with a group of five young women called, "The Kitty Kats." She was always grateful to her father for having made it possible for her to get this chance to be a dancer. Her mother had been afraid to allow her to go to Philadelphia but her father had said, "Let her go. If we don't give her her chance, she'll never forgive us."

My mother felt she deserved better from the world than she got, largely because she had been born in a nice building in The Bronx while most of the people who lived in our neighborhood (Highbridge—near Yankee Stadium) had been born in Europe or on the Lower East Side. And perhaps she was right. Perhaps everyone in her generation deserved better. They had come of age in the dream-generating 1920s only to find themselves entering ten years of depression followed by five years of war.

Yes, maybe this generation did deserve better. But how can one judge? Where is the standard of measurement? Perhaps the generation before them deserved better than World War One. Perhaps my father's dead parents deserved better than the pogroms they suffered in Russia before they emigrated to the U.S. And perhaps they deserved better than the Lower East Side when they got here. Perhaps everyone who ever lived deserved better. I don't know. Take it up with God. I only work here.

Chapter 2

One of my earliest memories is of one of the rare days I spent with my father. I was sitting on the stoop in front of our apartment house in the southwest Bronx, waiting for my father to come pick me up. Nelson Avenue was still a two-way street. After the war, when everyone bought a car, and a big car at that, most of the side streets in The Bronx would have to be converted to one-way streets, which was good for us kids since it made it easier for us to watch for cars and to play stickball in the street at the same time.

I didn't have to wait long. My father pulled up in a 1940 Plymouth, khaki, with a big white star on each of the two doors. An army car. He had borrowed it from his "place." My father wasn't in the Army so this was the closest I would get to feeling like I had a hero for a dad.

"Just a minute," my father said to me, as I came up to the car. "Anyone around?"

I knew he meant "any of my enemies." I looked up and down the block as he did. It was still early in the morning. The street was fairly deserted.

"I don't see anyone, Pop."

"OK. I've got some stuff to drop off."

He went to the trunk of his car, removed a carton, hid it under an army blanket, and walked into the cellar with me following. Since my grandfather owned the building, we had a private locked storeroom there. The dark, cool, musty room, laced with spider webs, was piled with stacks of cartons, six or seven high, all covered by army blankets.

"I got peas today." My father smiled. "Canned peas." He set the carton down on top of a tall pile. "They'll never starve me out."

"Who's that, Dad?"

"The hoarders."

"The hoarders?"

"Yeah, jerks that buy up everything so there's nothing left for anyone else. But don't you worry. They'll never starve my family. We can hold out for months, here."

I felt proud of my father. Of his foresight and the way he had provided for us. As we drove to his place, I asked him, "Daddy, why is everyone killing each other?"

"I don't know . . ."

"Well, I had this idea . . ."

"Oh, yeah?" He looked at me. Smiled. "What's that?"

"Why don't they all sign a treaty? Then no one would be allowed to fight anymore."

My father started to laugh. He ran his fingers through the thick, brown, curly hair on my big head. I could tell he was happy for a change and he felt good toward me, and we were together, me and my pop, in an army car, and we were going to his place, and somehow the problem of the Nazis, which I worried about sometimes, even though I was only five, somehow all problems seemed very far away.

"Don't you worry about anything anyhow," my father said, as we headed toward the East Bronx. "Do you know what I would do if anyone ever laid a hand on you? Do you have any idea what I would do if someone on the block laid a hand on you?"

"What Dad? What would you do?"

"I would kill them," he said, quietly. "If anyone, and I mean *anyone*, so much as laid one single hand on you, I would kill them," he added, looking into my eyes as we waited at a stoplight. When the light changed, he stepped on the gas and turned away, saying, "Do you know that? Do you know what I would do?"

"Yes, Dad," I said, shyly.

"What? What would I do?" he asked in a happy voice.

"Kill them?" I said, slightly embarrassed.

"You're damn right I would," he said with paternal pride. He rubbed my head again. "I'd kill anyone who touched you."

My father was like a spring that was wound too tight. He lived within taut self-restraints that were always on the edge of snapping. He believed he'd been taken advantage of all his life—by his bosses, by the vicissitudes of the economy, by the people on the Lower East Side, by fate, by accident, by everything. To his mind, he'd never gotten a fair shake. As an indigent orphan with a ninth grade education he'd had to fight for himself. He saw himself as an orphan even though his mother had remained alive for several years after his father. His mother did not speak English and was not able to help him very much when he entered the world which he saw as a jungle filled with his enemies. He was determined not to let anyone take advantage of what he saw as his "good nature." Sometimes, however, he carried this too far.

As we turned onto Tremont Avenue, my father began to talk about a man named Mr. Bukowski whom he had worked with on Staten Island. Pop had spent most of the war commuting to Fort Totten on Staten Island. He'd only been transferred to The Bronx in the past year. He'd left the house at six in the morning and returned home at eight at night for as long as I could remember. I hardly ever saw him. He spent Sundays, his only day off, with my grandfather who was teaching him the real estate business.

I rolled my window all the way down and rested my chin on the window rim, watching the stores on Tremont Avenue pass by. A car pulled up behind us, travelling at high speed on the virtually empty street. It tailgated us for a second.

"You see what I mean, Danny? Mr. Bukowski said you take the other side, you put yourself in the other guy's shoes . . ." The car behind us pulled out, passed us on the wrong side of the street, and swung quickly back into the lane right in front of us. ". . . and then you'll never have to . . . DID YOU SEE THAT? DID YOU *SEE* THAT? HE CUT ME OFF! THAT SON OF A BITCH CUT ME OFF!"

My father gripped the wheel as if he were trying to choke it and slammed on the gas, throwing me back in my seat as the car lurched forward. He began to chase the other car along the street at a dangerous pace that sent pedestrians scurrying.

My father's chin jutted out revealing his lower teeth and his face took on a demonic expression as he raced after the other car, moving forward in his seat until he was practically up against the steering wheel which he held tightly with two hands like a machine gun. He ran a light, passed the other car by careening down the wrong side of the street, then swung suddenly to the right causing our tires to scream and throwing us into the path of the other driver who slammed on his brakes to avoid crashing into my door. He swerved violently to the right along with us, both cars running into the curb with tire squeals and a bump. My father flung open his door and as the other man, a young man, perhaps twenty-five, with a puzzled, astonished look, tried to get out of his car, my father was upon him, at his throat, attempting to choke him, throwing him to the street and falling on top of him. The man grabbed at my father's throat as my father growled, "You cut me off." They rolled around, each on top of the other in the gutter like two dogs at each other's throats until two trucks and a car stopped and two men got out of each truck and a man out of the car and the men ran over. Most of the men were bigger than my father. They pulled my father and the man he had attacked off each other.

"He's a madman," the young guy said, not resisting the truck drivers. "He's nuts. I'm telling you. That guy's a nut." He massaged his throat where my father had choked him.

"He cut me off," my father said. "That son of a bitch cut me off."

I sat in the car, frozen by a combination of excitement and terror as a middle-aged black man with a friendly expression moved off the sidewalk into the street. He picked up my father's glasses which hadn't broken, and his bow tie which had been torn off. The young man wanted no more of my father. He turned to look at his car, at the tires where he'd hit the curb, more to get out of the situation than to seek for real damage. My father quickly calmed down and became the paymaster again, the young son-in-law of a landlord. Everyone relaxed as the black man handed my father his glasses, and he put them on. The man then took my father's tie and began to dust it with his hand and this gesture further calmed my father down.

I moved unobtrusively out of the car and into the gutter which, though normally forbidden territory, was now safe with all the traffic stopped and everyone standing around in the street, so I knew I could take this little exciting liberty and be there with the men. The black man handed my father his bow tie. As the kid got back into his car and backed out into the street, my father clipped his tie on, saying to the friendly black man in a strangely quiescent voice, "He cut me off." The black man shook his shoulders as he laughed and said, "I knows it, but you can't be chokin' folks in the street now," and my father said, quietly, "Well . . . that son of a bitch shouldn't'a cut me off." The black man nodded his head and continued to smile as he began to lightly swat some of the street grime off the back of father's shirt, saying, softly, "No . . . You can't be chokin' the whole world, can you now?" But I could see that he liked my father, he seemed to *understand* my father in some profound, empathic way, and it was as if although he himself couldn't choke the world, not with his black skin, he could very easily sympathize with, and even identify with, someone who had actually made the attempt, if only in a symbolic way, in a single, particular circumstance.

I looked around at the other men. They were all amused by my father. They displayed a large tolerance toward his actions, and even, perhaps, a certain affinity for the way he had behaved.

As for myself, in my own life I would not find the question of the use of force, of the turning to violence in response to perceived provocation or even in self-defense, so easy to resolve.

Chapter 3

On Friday nights, my mother's family got together at her parents' apartment next door to ours, for the Sabbath dinner. The building we lived in was U-shaped, six floors high, made of tan brick. You entered the main lobby through a courtyard flanked by bushes on either side, and then you went to the right or left side of the building, each with twenty apartments and its own staircase. We lived in the front, on the right side, on the first floor, just above Blum's "Home Cooking," which you entered directly from the street.

I liked to get to my grandparents' apartment early on Friday evenings to watch my grandmother cover her head with a linen napkin and sway in the corner as she mumbled in Hebrew and lit the Sabbath candles. Then my grandfather opened up the large, expandable dining room table in the living room, and we gathered for dinner—my parents, myself, my Uncle Bernie, his wife Bessie, his son Louie the Mook (my cousin, almost a year older than I), his daughter (my cousin) Carol, who was my age, and my mother's unmarried sister, Rose. We three kids sat at a bridge table next to the large table. My baby brother, Barry, slept in his carriage in the next room.

My grandmother began by serving the gefilte fish which we kids didn't like—except for my cousin Louie, who would eat anything. Later, in high school, Louie was the only Jewish kid who bought hot dogs from Rocco, the old Italian man who sold them covered with onions in tomato sauce from his little pushcart with a gold and blue umbrella. Rocco had two missing fingers on his left hand which had contracted into a kind of rigid claw. He used it to hold the hot dog roll while he smeared on the onions. He also used it as a holder when he pissed against the side of the school between customers.

I liked eating at my grandparents' apartment. My father never went out of control there. My grandfather was teaching his son-in-law the real estate business, and my father was extremely respectful and almost reverent when in his presence.

My Uncle Bernie, who was my grandfather's own son, was a different story entirely.

My grandfather began the dinner conversation, as usual, on a religious note. "So how's business?" he said to Bernie.

"Not bad. Ida is letting me do the buying now." Bernie chewed a matzo along with his fish. My grandmother went into the kitchen to get some more horseradish.

"Why you want to work for a woman, I don't know," my grandfather said. "That wasn't the case in my day. In my day, a man who was a man didn't work for a woman."

"There's other advantages to it," Bernie said with a leer.

My Aunt Bessie continued to eat her fish, pretending not to have caught Bernie's implication. My grandfather gave Bernie a fierce look. "This is the Sabbath," he said, with a finality which implied, "Mess up tonight and you not only insult me and your mother, you insult the laws of Moses, the future nation of Israel, and the Jewish people as a whole, whether living or dead, here or abroad, mentioned in the Bible or not."

My Uncle Bernie returned to his fish without replying. My grandfather patted my father, who was sitting next to him, on the back. "My son-in-law Sid doesn't work for a woman."

Bernie was trying to remain silent, but he couldn't resist saying, "No, he works for the government for such a stinkin' salary he can't even afford to give my sister an apartment in an elevator building."

"We live on the first floor," my father said. "Right next to the front door."

"Floor, schmoor," Bernie said. "It's the principle of the matter. My sister deserves better."

"I don't live in an elevator building either," my grandfather said, in a manner which indicated that he believed this ended the argument in my father's favor.

Bessie and Rose and my mother stifled their giggles.

"Funny, uh?" my grandfather said. "You think I'm funny, uh?" They didn't look up.

"Sha, Ben, Sha," my grandmother said, coming in with another dish of celery and black olives.

My grandfather gave her a dirty look. Then he said to Bernie, "I don't know how you can get anywhere at a job like that."

"Maybe I should run your buildings for you."

My grandfather laughed. "That'll be the day. Sid, Sid can run my buildings. You . . . the tenants would walk all over you . . ."

"Yeah, Sid . . . Sid's a sick man."

My mother and father straightened up with a jolt.

"Sid isn't a sick man," my mother said.

"Are you kidding? When you first married him and moved him into the building he couldn't stop coughing. You don't want to remember now, do you? How do you think it looked for the rest of us? All the tenants were talking about Pop behind his back. Saying his daughter married a sick man."

"We went to Dr. Stern and got him certified," my mother said. "Don't tell me sick man! Dr. Stern, he said himself, Sid had a disease, yes, but a sick man, no."

"That's what he said," my father added. "That's the God's truth. I was sick but I wasn't any sick man."

"Bernie, lay off," my Aunt Bessie said.

"Yeah, yeah . . ." Bernie said.

"You're just jealous," my father said. He turned to my grandfather. "When the war broke out he tried for three years to get my disease. He broke his neck trying to catch it. But I didn't have to do a thing. I already had it." He laughed. "Then when the induction notices came, we saw who was the sick man." He turned toward my Uncle Bernie. "Your father had to buy your way out. And I was out already. I didn't cost him a single penny."

"Buy my way out? He didn't buy my way out."

"Sha. Eat, eat," my grandmother said, picking up the plates from those who were finished with their fish.

"He doesn't wanna work anyhow," my father said, adding sarcastically, "He thinks he oughta be in the movies."

"He could be in the movies," my Aunt Bessie said, "if only he

20

got a break."

"I'll give him a break," my grandfather said. "I'll break his arm."

My Aunt Rose laughed, more at my grandfather than at his joke.

My grandfather turned toward her. "You think your father is funny, hah? You . . . Twenty-seven years old and not even married yet."

"Pa . . . ," my mother pleaded, "don't talk about her age . . . The kids . . . Someone could hear . . ."

"I should have grandchildren from her already. She should have been married five years ago."

"I could've been married," Rose said. "Rhett Butler proposed to me but I turned him down. I didn't like his gambling."

"Who? Red the Butler?" my grandfather said. "Who's this Red the Butler?"

"A southerner," my Uncle Bernie said. "He was wild over her."

"A butler?" my grandfather said again. He turned toward my Aunt Rose. "You're seeing a butler?" My aunt laughed. He turned toward Bernie. "He's Jewish, this butler?"

"He runs around with this *shiksa*, Scarlett O'Hara," my uncle said.

"O'Hara!" my grandfather shouted. "Irish! You're running around with a man who's running around with the Irish?"

At this everyone but my father cracked up. My grandfather looked to my father who explained, "They're just kidding you, Pop. It's in a movie."

"Kidding?" my grandfather said, his anger rising. "*Kidding?*" He turned toward Bernie and raised his hand as if he was about to smite the table.

"Oh, oh, Pop's playing ping-pong again," Bernie said, and all the women giggled because whenever my grandfather became angry at his son at the table he raised his hand and held it in the air, flat and shaking slightly, as if he were about to serve a ping-pong ball. He did this in two ways: backhand or forehand.

"A forehand," Bernie said, as everyone continued to laugh. There was an ozone smell in the air. My grandfather's temper was beginning to glow. Yet he was somewhat puzzled by all this. He was not sure what was going on with this "ping-pong." He was trying to fit all this into Yiddish terms so he could figure out how to deal with it. But he couldn't. There was no Yiddish word for "ping-pong."

"Sha, Sha," my grandmother said, patting him on the shoulder with her left hand while serving him chicken soup with matzo balls with her right. The steam engine of Pop's anger continued to simmer but he didn't put it into gear. He began to eat his soup as my grandmother served the other adults. My mother and Bessie cleared the remaining gefilte fish plates from the table and served soup to us kids at our little bridge table. We were all giggling too, not completely sure at what we were giggling, until my grandfather silenced us with a look.

"You'll go far," my grandfather said to my uncle, sarcastically. "Working for a woman in a Victrola record store."

"At least it's better than wasting my time at the government, like Sid."

"Wasting my time?" my father said. "I don't waste my time."

"No? Whaddya do there?"

"I steal."

"Steal?" Bernie said contemptuously. "*You* steal?"

"I steal everything that isn't tied down," my father said, proudly.

"He's lying, Pa. He doesn't steal," my mother said.

"You see!" Bernie said.

"Sha! Sha!" my grandfather said to Bernie while pointing to my father with his thumb. "Sid's gonna get ahead after the war. Not like you. You're a good for nothing."

"Jesus Christ, Pop," my uncle said, "will ya lay off?"

"Jee . . . Jee . . ." My grandfather could hardly speak. He was choking on a matzo ball. "Did he say . . . Did he say that name in my house?"

He lifted his hand to take a swat at Bernie but my grandmother grabbed his arm. "Don't you mention that name in my house," he said, calming down somewhat.

I leaned over toward my mother and tapped her on the back. She turned toward me. "Mommy, who's Jesus?" I whispered.

"A Jewish man. Long ago. He wanted to be a big shot so he said he was God and all the dumb *goyem* believed him. Ever since then they've been killing us because of him."

My uncle sipped at his soup but his face was red. I knew he was going to speak. "You shouldn't hit me, Pa," he said. "I'm thirty-four years old now. I'm a grown man."

"A man!" my grandfather snorted. "A man!" He looked Bernie in the eye. "Can you swim from Coney Island to Brighton Beach?"

"*What?*" Bernie said, beginning to smile along with my mother and Rose. They had heard this twenty times before.

"From Coney Island to Brighton. Can you swim from Coney Island to Brighton Beach?" my grandfather said. "And you call yourself a man!" He said this proudly, but he was surprised to see that, except for my father and grandmother, all the rest of us, kids and adults, were laughing at him. His ears began to flush with anger.

"Listen to this one," my uncle said to those of us who were laughing with him. "Je . . . a . . . Gee Whiz and Moses are at Coney Island. They're going to have a miracle contest. All the bathers are gathered around. They're going to walk on water. Three times the two of them try. Three times Moses does it. And each time Gee Whiz sinks. Finally, Gee Whiz turns to Moses and he says, 'Tell me, three times we tried this and three times you did it. The whole crowd is going crazy for you. Cheering and applauding. Tell me, what's the secret?' And Moses turns to him and he whispers in his ear, 'Step on the rocks, *schmuck!*' "

Everyone exploded into laughter, but my grandfather leaped to his feet yelling, " '*Schmuck!*' You say '*schmuck*' in my house on the Sabbath?" He reached across the table, trying to swat Bernie with a quick forehand and backhand, but the table was large and Bernie was too nimble, leaping up and scrambling behind his chair, and then, as my grandfather leaned over the table to try to reach him, my uncle started to do a kind of Charlie Chaplin ballet, yelling, "Ping-pong, ping-pong," and every time my grandfather swung at him, my uncle avoided the slap by jerking his head back and then pretended to be returning a ping-pong shot.

By this time, when we kids were practically out of our minds with glee and my Aunt Rose was laughing so hard she could scarcely breathe, my grandfather began an end run around the table to kill Bernie once and for all, but my grandmother stepped in his path and started to wail and do her shot-bear routine back and forth in front of him as he tried to get past her. My uncle turned white with fear. My grandfather, in frustration, grabbed the side of the table with both his hands and turned the entire table over on my uncle and my mother and my Aunt Bessie, chicken soup all over everyone, matzo balls flying, olives rolling, my grandmother crying, we kids squealing, and my grandfather growled and turned around and stomped out of the house

with my father on his tail, saying, "Take it easy, Pop . . . Take it easy."
As they stormed through the doorway, they passed Blum, running
up from his restaurant. He was wearing a long white apron, his face
stricken as he said, politely, to my crying grandmother, "Mrs. Farber,
please Mrs. Farber. I can't run a restaurant this way. The customers.
They're getting plaster in their soup."

My grandmother just sat on the couch weeping and dazed, looking at her matzo ball soup all over everything and her huge dining
room table, listing on its side like the great ocean liner *Normandie,* which
had caught fire and rolled over in New York harbor.

Chapter 4

Like any war, World War Two wasn't all action. Much of the time was spent sitting around, filling the clock-space with the chatter of wishes and regrets.

I remember one steamy afternoon in late spring. The rain had stopped for a while and we sat at the open window in my bedroom, my mother and I, looking out at the slick street. The one tree on our block was still standing. It hadn't been knocked down yet by a monstrous hurricane near the end of the war.

My Aunt Rose was sprawled on my bed, thumbing through a movie magazine. She went to the movies often. It started when she was supposed to be attending Theodore Roosevelt High School on East Fordham Road. East Fordham Road was Fordham Baldie territory when I was in high school. There were many outsiders who had seen this area in the daytime, but few who had seen it at night and returned to the West Bronx to tell about it.

But that wasn't my aunt's problem when she had gone to high school. My aunt's problem was that the bus which was supposed to transport her to school also went to the intersection of Fordham Road and the Grand Concourse which was proximate to five movie theaters. She had rarely made it to school.

Her favorite theater was the Loew's Paradise, the showplace of The Bronx. A huge movie palace, it was designed to resemble an ancient castle with tall turrets on either side of the screen under a dark blue sky caparisoned with little twinkling electric stars in the ceiling. We always believed, when we were kids, that there were clouds floating across this sky, although now I don't see how they could have done that. But perhaps they did. In any case, the Loew's Paradise was high school, college, and graduate school for my aunt, since she went there often during the day for years.

My aunt stretched out there on my bed, wearing white bobby sox, black flats, a full red skirt, a pink sleeveless sweater, and a red ribbon in her long, dark hair cut in bangs in the front. She was chubby in a fittingly baby-fat way since she was defined as the baby of the family. Her skin was light, her lipstick bright, and there was still a youthful prettiness about her, along with the incipient roundness in her features, a doll-like unformedness around a core of passivity that was revealed by the way she had plopped herself down on the bed.

An old ice truck ground its way up the wet street to unload blocks of ice for Blum's Restaurant. On the radio, Jo Stafford sang, "I'll Be Seeing You." Then my mother broke the silence between us in the heavy spring air by saying, languorously, "I don't know . . . Maybe I should've married Davey Bernstein. He owns a fruit store now. Over on Featherbed Lane. He's getting ahead in the world."

"At least you're married," my aunt said.

"Don't talk that way! You could be married, too."

"Oh, yeah . . . I was going to marry Ronald Colman, you know, as soon as he finished his last film, but with the U-boats and all, he can't get over here for the wedding . . . The fuckin' U-boats!" she added, laughing.

"*Rose!*" my mother said. She was trying to appear shocked, but she couldn't stifle a tiny giggle. "You're still young yet . . . Look, maybe you could marry Fat Willie Baumholtz," she said, joking, knowing this would get her sister to do her Fat Willie Baumholtz imitation, and it did, my aunt leaping up and giggling and waddling around the room like Fat Willie. When she returned to the bed, Rose said, "Fat Willie! If he ever took off that Yankee hat he wears all the time, his head would probably come off with it . . . He's a bigger loser than I am."

"You're not a loser," my mother said. "Really . . ." But they didn't go into it.

My mother took out her scrapbook, as she often did, and showed me her medals for girls' basketball at Roosevelt High, and the pictures of her, athletic, lively, with dark bangs over big, dark, hopeful, eyes. Pictures of her as a lovely cheerleader; as a dancer in Philadelphia; on the rail of a ship with her skirt up a bit, in *The Bronx Home News*— "Bronx Lass Returns For Show Biz Career." ("They made it up. I just went down to the ship with this photographer I was dating. He works for *The Daily News* now. I could have married *him*. He's a big man, now.") Pictures of her with various men, alone or doubling with my Aunt Bessie. "Remember this guy, Rose?" She held the album up. My aunt nodded yes. "He's a lawyer, now." She turned to me. "He would've married me in a second. I could have married a big man." Finally, she turned to a photo of her and my father sitting in a rowboat. "But I picked your father."

Another old truck pulled up to the curb. Loaded with seltzer bottles that you squirted like fire extinguishers. A man walked up the middle of the street leading a horse and wagon. "High-cash clothes! High-cash clothes!"

It began to drizzle again. My mother sat quietly, looking into the distance, dreaming. Then she said to me, softly, "Your father . . . You see, he's not like you or me, Danny . . . You and me, we're more sensitive people. He comes from the Lower East Side . . . Did you know my grandmother was famous in Europe for reading? In her whole town in Europe, whenever anyone had a problem, they came to her with it. All day, she sat by the window, reading the Bible. And you know . . . you take after her. Even my mother always says so. Doesn't she, Rose?"

My aunt looked up from her movie magazine and nodded yes. The Andrews Sisters sang, "Don't Sit Under The Apple Tree," in the background. My mother continued, "And it's true. You do. You do take after me. After *my* family. The Farbers. We're sensitive people. Your father's different. He's not a fine person . . . Not like you and me . . ."

It began to rain harder. The news came on the radio. Eleanor Roosevelt was speaking about freedom and the prairies and the mountains of America. My mother, who was the consummate American dreamer, was carried along on the waves of glorious rhetoric. Tears came into her eyes as always when she heard someone intone the majesties of America, while my Aunt Rose, who was already beginning to understand that success might not be a journey which was meant for her in this lifetime, and that there was a good chance she was going to be one of the potential diamonds left behind as detritus of the American dream, my Aunt Rose began to laugh and to mimic Eleanor Roosevelt, parading around the room with a stern expression and spouting out in a falsetto voice, "Boy Scouts of Amurrikkka . . ."

And yet, one day, in 1945, I would come home to find both of them in the kitchen, crying.

"What happened, Mommy? What's wrong?"

"President Roosevelt died, Danny. President Roosevelt died," and she burst into sobs as she said it. She wiped her eyes with a hankie. Blew her nose. Tried to control herself. "He was good to the Jews, Danny. He was good to the Jews."

My aunt slumped there on a chair in the corner, weeping.

A few months later, the larger world interposed on the small circle of my life once again. My Cousin Herbie, who was a year older than I, came up to me in front of our building and told me there was some new kind of bomb we had dropped. Something like a "Tom Mix" bomb.

When Herbie's father, my Uncle Lenny, split off from a group of men who had been talking animatedly on the corner and walked toward our building, we intercepted him.

"That's right, boys," he replied to our question. "They call it an atomic bomb. That's what everyone's talkin' about. It can blow up a whole city."

"In one shot?" Herbie said.

"You know it, boys," Lenny said, buoyantly. "The war's gonna be over now. You watch and see."

"It is, Uncle Lenny?"

"That's right. And boys, I want you to remember this day. They said on the radio this is going to be the turning point in history. God, I only wish I was your age."

"Why is that, Pop?" Herbie said.

"Because, boys, this bomb is made out of the power of the sun. And that power can do anything." My uncle was filled with the fire of exuberance and grand feeling. "When you grow up, boys, you'll have all kinds of new things. Airplanes. Everything."

"I'll have my own airplane?" I said.

"Why not? Then you can live in the country and fly to work.

28

And listen, boys, one teaspoon of this atomic stuff is so powerful it can air-condition the whole city of New York. Believe me, when you boys grow up, you won't be sitting on hot fire escapes in the middle of the night because your house is like a sweatbox and it's drivin' you crazy."

"Hey, no one's gonna mess with us now!" Herbie said. "If the Nazis or the Japs try anything now—WHAMMO!"

"That's right, boys. That's the best part of it. There'll be no more wars now. There's only three people who can even understand this bomb. Einstein and two other scientists. And they're not gonna tell anyone how to make it." He nodded to my grandfather who passed us on the sidewalk. "I only wish they had it a few years sooner. Then Phil Blumenthal, my friend who lived up in 4C, would still be alive." My uncle was somber suddenly. "Listen, boys, don't ever underestimate the power of America. The Germans and the Japs underestimated us, but we showed 'em. This is a great country and we can do anything if we put our minds to it."

When I went into my apartment, I told my mother and my Aunt Rose about the new bomb.

". . . and Uncle Lenny says it can blow up a whole city in one shot!"

"In one shot?" my mother said.

"That's what Uncle Lenny said."

My Aunt Rose giggled and said, "Hey, maybe we can get them to drop it on Rifkin, across the air shaft, when he sings off key with the window open."

Chapter 5

It had been fifteen years of hardship for the people on our block. Fifteen years in the wilderness—difficult years during which they felt deserted by the object of their worship: Fifteen years without BUYING. But after the war, as goods became available and money was plentiful, BUYING returned and people did the great god proper homage.

My mother and Muriel Teitner were two of his most devoted followers. They began a kind of competition for his favors. They went to his local temples, they made offerings of precious paper, and they brought home evidence of their devotion. New furniture for the living room, new beds, drapes, a car, a fur coat.

Whenever Muriel would buy something, my mother would say to my father, "Who does she think she is? My father is the landlord. Do you know what a landlord means? It means 'the lord of the land.' " So my father would buy my mother something more expensive. And then Muriel would say to her husband, "Who does she think she is? Just because her father's the landlord. Her husband's just a guy from the Lower East Side. And you own your own radio-repair shop already." And the bout would move to the next round, and my father would lose six more hairs from his head with each purchase.

Yet I can't say this was an imposition on my father. A dream alone is like masturbation. It is only when two people dream the same dream that the dream glows with the full eroticism of reality. The dream of "Daughter of the Lord of the Land" required a prince as well as a princess. And my father was quite willing to apply for this role. And if becoming a prince meant one would have to be a frog for a while, well that was fine with him too.

But I have to admit the immediate post-war years were not easy for my father. Fate seemed determined to put obstacles in his way. For instance, fate decreed at about this time that there should appear parking meters at the big shopping area on 170th Street. This meant my father could no longer park his car there. He had to drop us off and then drive to another street to try to find a parking place. After all, was it becoming to a citizen of a free country to pay a penny to park his car on a public street?

Years later, when my father finally did have money, and he and my mother lived in Westchester, he continued his unwavering support for this principle of free streets, which he seemed to believe was guaranteed by the Bill of Rights. He devised intricate routes to beat the tolls on the New York State Thruway and the Saw Mill River Parkway. God only knows how much time and gas money he spent on the detours he would make, over hill and dale, hither and yon, to avoid *ever* having to pay a quarter to drive on a road.

By the late 1940s, my father was serving in effect as my grandfather's personal secretary, reading his correspondence to him, writing out his answers, and keeping his books. My grandfather rewarded him by taking him in as a partner in buying an apartment house across the street. My father, with his Lower East Side background and his ninth grade education, was still worried about where his next meal was coming from and feared having to go back to sweeping movie theaters. Because of my grandfather's generosity, however, my father wound up on the bottom of a twenty-five-thousand dollar mortgage.

"Don't worry," my grandfather would say. "The rents will exactly pay off the mortgage."

"I know," my father would say. "I know."

And he did know. Morning, noon, and night, he knew, as the figures of dollars and cents, rents and notes due, raced through his worried brain.

At this point in my life society was attempting to socialize me by sending me to a factory each day. They called this factory a school.

I was always a good student. Learning came easy to me and I liked to learn. But I never liked school. It seemed like having a job and not getting paid for it.

They dressed us like little businessmen each day. First with knickers and starched shirts, then with regular trousers and white shirt and blue tie for assembly on Tuesday. Well, I never cared much for being like everyone else. It wasn't my idea of a thrill to be in a concrete schoolyard with 800 other kids, all dressed alike, marching around in groups as bells rang to tell us what to do.

Albert Einstein said about parades, how can people enjoy putting one foot after the other in unison? And Albert Einstein was revered in our neighborhood. He was seen as the Jew who won the war since most people believed he had invented the atom bomb.

My trouble at school began back during the war on the day I was supposed to enter kindergarten. My mother took me there, and I'd been looking forward to it, but when I got to the place, the cruel, square, white-brick, five-story, mausoleum in which I was supposed to spend the rest of the days of my youth, I balked. It seemed like a box to me. I thought they were trying to shut me up in a box. But they didn't call it putting me in a box. They called it education.

Well, I just dug in my heels. I wouldn't take another step. My mother was in a dilemma, because in the family movie my father was the wicked and strict disciplinarian while she was too soft to deal with the world and was always being taken advantage of by everyone— especially by me. Yet I *did* have to go to school.

My mother thought of the answer: "Come with me, Danny."

I knew I'd been trumped, but what could I do? I skulked along after her as she crossed the street and went to the pay phone in the rear of a candy store, where she called my father and explained the situation to him. Then she put me on the line and my father explained the alternative: "Danny, you have two choices. Either you go to school right now like everyone else, or, number two, I'm going to have to go to my boss and get permission to leave my place, and then I'm going to go to my car, and then I'm going to drive all the way over there, and then I'm going to beat the living daylights out of you. Now which will it be?"

"I'll go to school, Dad," I said, quietly, and as I handed the receiver to my mother, I could hear my father's voice in the receiver, in a racking shout like a little gnome having a fit, "You'd better go to school, smart guy, before I come over there and break your goddamn neck . . ."

My mother took a few minutes to calm him down, and then to tell me how lucky I was to have a soft person like herself to protect me from an insensitive maniac like my father, but shortly thereafter we proceeded on to the school. The schoolyard was empty by the time we got there so we went up to my class on the second floor. The teacher came to greet us at the door. Her whole face was bandaged and raw.

"Hello. I'm Mrs. Ratsky," she said. Then she saw me looking up at her mangled face. "Oh, don't mind this, Danny," she explained. "I was just bitten in the face by a dog." She reached down for my hand, saying, "Just come this way now, Danny. You can leave now, Mrs. Schwartz."

I quickly leapt back and headed for the stairs. My mother grabbed me and got me in a kind of hammerlock while Mrs. Ratsky tried to help her and to keep her eye on the rest of the class inside at the same time. I began to scream and Mrs. Ratsky said, "Danny! Please be quiet or Miss Mann will hear. Her office is right down the hall."

I continued to tug and fight because I knew this Miss McMann who was the principal's secretary. She'd had dealings with my grandfather and she was a small, very nice, meek woman whom I didn't fear in the least. However, what I didn't realize was that Mrs. Ratsky said Miss Mann and not Miss McMann, and Miss Mann was the principal and she weighed two hundred and twenty pounds, and she was coming down the hallway at me. The principal, aimed at me.

The rest of the scene was inexorably traumatic. I froze. My mother froze. Miss Mann picked me up under her left arm as if I were a sack of barley for mushroom and barley soup at Blum's. At the same time she placed her huge right paw on my mother's back and pushed her into the stairwell, saying, "Thank you, madam. You won't be needed any more. I'll take over." I could see the frightened look on my mother's face as Miss Mann carried me into the room and deposited me on an empty seat. She looked into my eyes and said, "That will be enough. Do you understand?"

I nodded yes. I understood. She was right. It *was* enough for me. I wasn't going to go through this again for a while. It was not the most auspicious beginning for my life in the larger world of American social institutions.

In the second grade I had another day of panic which resulted in another call to my father and another death threat which convinced me that I would rather deal with school than with him. But that night, in a way which wasn't consciously intended, I got him back.

It was early on a spring evening, shortly after the war. My father was sitting in just his bathrobe with the bridge table opened up over his legs as he stretched back in his easy chair and read *The Bronx Home News*. My mother was in the kitchen washing the dishes. I was on the floor with my brother across the room from my father. We were coloring with crayons in coloring books.

Then I got an exciting idea. I looked under the table and saw my father's crotch. Wouldn't it be fun to sneak up to him (he wouldn't see me coming because I'd crawl under the table) and give his balls a tweak? He'd be so surprised because he hadn't seen me and he'd appreciate my skill in surprising him in that way, and we'd share a laugh together.

I snuck up on him, and just as I thought, he didn't even notice I was in the room, much less that I was slithering toward him, hidden from view by the bridge table and his newspaper. I made it right up to him under the table. He still didn't see me. I could hardly bear it, it was so perfect and everything had gone so well, and then I reached up and just gave his balls a little squeeze . . .

Well, I guess I squeezed a little too hard. In fact, I know I squeezed a little too hard. I knew it the moment I did it, because my father gave out a stupefying kamikaze roar and flew up into the air (and I mean *flew*) like he'd been hit with a tremendous electric shock, and Bang! the bridge table went flying over on the right, breaking one leg off as it landed, and my mother came running into the room, shouting in panic, "What happened? What *happened*?" as my father rolled around on the floor in agony, holding his balls and making these aggghhh! noises through his teeth, his face all twisted. My mother bent down to him, "Sid, Sid," as he said through his tight bitten teeth, "I'll kill him. I'll kill him."

Well, I didn't need a jury of twelve responsible citizens to tell me to get the hell out of there. I ran upstairs as fast as I could and

34

hid in my Uncle Lenny's apartment. I never was good at lying, especially to people I liked, so when he asked me what had happened, I had to tell him. Uncle Lenny had a big dropped wrestler's chest and heavy arms with tattoos on them and a thick bald head. When he began to laugh you knew he was laughing. Now, he roared. He grabbed my aunt who was in the kitchen with their son, Herbie, saying, "Fanny, come on, you got to see this." The three of them ran downstairs with me following. I couldn't remain upstairs by myself without my uncle to protect me. We ran into my family's apartment, and there was my father, still sitting on the floor, holding his balls, a bewildered grimace on his face, looking like a monkey.

My uncle had told my aunt what had happened as they ran down the stairs and they began to howl with laughter. My father looked up at them, embarrassed. He realized the absurdity of his position. A hint of a smile revealed itself on his face as he said, "Very funny! Very funny!" trying to be serious, but my aunt and uncle just laughed even louder, and my mother joined in, and I realized I was going to get out alive once again.

Chapter 6

My Cousin Herbie, the son of Uncle Lenny and Aunt Fanny, was my closest friend. Like my Cousin Louie, he was a year older than I. Herbie could be seen as either a bright, precocious, verbal, witty, spirited little kid, or a little wise-ass, big-mouthed kid, depending on whether you were his mother or not.

To Aunt Fanny, Herbie was always right. She was ready to defend him in every altercation. Once he insulted Fat Lena Peskin. Lena had yelled at him, "If you were my son, I'd kill you!" Herbie had replied, "Lady, if you were my mother, I'd kill *myself.*"

Herbie had always been a bit odd in his behavior. When he was little, and the women were sitting outside rocking their carriages, sometimes he would run up to them and shout, "Cocky-doody!" for no reason at all, and then run away. Often he came into our apartment when my parents weren't home and jumped up and down on their bed, until one day my father caught him in the act, and chased him out of the house and down the street, hitting him with a broom. When he was ten, he rebelled against his father, a fiercely loyal Yankee rooter, by becoming the block's only Dodger fan.

Uncle Lenny had a great deal of free time, since he worked irregularly. Most of the time he hung around the block and played ball with the kids and took us places. He never had much money, but he always had enough for his family to get by. Every six months or so he would go off on a business trip for a week or two. He seemed to make sufficient money from this to survive.

I would have loved it if my father had been around more, but I think Herbie would have wanted his father to have a regular job. Herbie was always dissatisfied and he was usually depressed.

Uncle Lenny loved to play stickball with us. When we were in junior high, my Cousin Louie would come to our block, and Louie and I would play my uncle and my brother Barry in fast-pitch every afternoon. My uncle even bought my brother a catcher's mask. He had all these strange pitches, my uncle did, and he had a Yiddish name for each one: "Watch it, here comes my matzo ball," or "Here comes my *eppes* pitch. Look out!"

Lenny's son, Herbie, however, generally stayed in his house. While his mother shopped and worked or sat with the women on the sidewalk, he would linger there by himself, listening to Dodger games on the radio or later, watching them on TV, cooking himself fried banana sandwiches.

Lenny tried to get Herbie involved in our games. Sometimes he succeeded, by trying to grab Herbie and wrestling him around. My uncle looked like a wrestler and he told us he had been one. "I once fought Ed 'Strangler' Lewis."

"You did, Uncle Lenny?"

"Sure. We used to work out in the gym together. I knew him so well I called him 'Ed.' Everyone else had to call him 'Mr. Lewis.'"

"Did he try to strangle you, Uncle Lenny?"

"Nah. That was just his name. He was a gentleman. A great man. But I would hold my own with him, I'll tell you." And at this point, he would give a sumo-wrestler roar and leap on Herbie and put a series of locks on his son, twirling Herbie around, rendering him helpless. Sometimes Herbie laughed and really loved what was happening, but other times he got angry and went upstairs by himself to sulk.

Uncle Lenny had a grand enthusiasm, a brimming basket of ideas for games and trips for us kids to take with him. He told exciting stories about stealing apples from pushcarts and running from the cops on the Lower East Side, jumping from roof to roof on the tenements, swinging across from one building to another on the clotheslines. Usually Herbie joined us and had a good time, but the trick was to get him out of bed and then to get him out of his house less than two hours later.

What was perhaps most amazing about my Uncle Lenny was his hobby. Here was this big burly man from the Lower East Side, usually wearing a white tee-shirt with his belly hanging over his belt and his tattoos revealed on his heavy arms, and when he had some spare time, he liked to sew. Every once in a while, in the evening, he would show up at our door, wearing half-spectacles, with a thimble on his finger, and he would sit down in our living room under the light and sew our torn clothes. My father could never understand it, but he didn't object or make a scene. What the hell, he must have thought, Lenny might be nuts but he saved us good money at the tailor's.

Unlike my uncle, my father hardly ever went to a baseball game. His philosophy was, Why pay for a game when you could hear it for free on the radio? After all, it was the same game, wasn't it? But he did have some free time for a while after the war, and at one point he began to take accordion lessons.

None of us could envision this working out too well, but he seemed to believe in it. He rented an accordion and he kept saying to me, "You see, Danny, if you play the piano and you go to a party, you can't bring a piano along. If they don't have a piano, you're stuck. But if you got an accordion, you just bring it along."

I didn't want to be the one to tell him he never went to parties anyhow. I figured if I left it alone, it would go away, and it did, a short time later, when he found that playing the accordion wasn't as simple as it had looked to him. He'd had dreams of going to parties and being surrounded by all these people as he played, "Lady of Spain." Everyone would be astonished when, on the second chorus, he would shake the accordion to create a vibrato effect, and one woman would say to another, "I didn't know he played so *well*," and the other would reply, admiringly, "And he picked it up so fast." But after a few weeks of running scales with his right hand and pressing the wrong buttons with his left, he gave it up. For a month or two thereafter, whenever I'd see him, he felt it necessary to justify this, I guess, because he'd always say to me, "You see, Danny, if you play the piano and you go to a party, you just sit down and play, see, and it's all right, but with an accordion, you see, you gotta bring it along with you . . . It don't look right, you know what I mean?"

And I would nod yes, and if we were outdoors, in the sunshine, he would take my chin in his hands and hold my face up to the light and begin to pick out blackheads, saying, "Hold still! I just don't like blackheads," as I tried to pull away.

Chapter **7**

In the years 1945 through 1948 the world was generally good to the people in our neighborhood. The boys were home, the peacetime economy began to be rebuilt, Western Europe began to be rebuilt, and the Yankees began to be rebuilt.

1948 was perhaps the best year of all. Of course, the Yankees finished sadly out of the money, but this was compensated for by the founding of the state of Israel. Everyone flew little blue and white flags with the Jewish star on them and things appeared to be going our way.

Even my father seemed relatively content. He continued to work hard after the war and then, in 1948, he bought a partnership in a liquor store in Spanish Harlem. In those days, for a person of our class, owning a liquor store was the equivalent of a medical degree for people on a higher social stratum. There were fixed prices so you were virtually guaranteed a profit, and since there were a fixed number of liquor licenses in New York State, and they had already been given out, no one could compete with you by opening a store nearby. By purchasing a liquor store, you were purchasing a steady income and respectability.

To purchase the store, my father merely had to pay $30,000. Now, in those days, $30,000 was BIG MONEY. And my father went into BIG DEBT. This, on top of the mortgage on the building he had bought with my grandfather. But he had his father-in-law behind him, and he had his dreams, his new respectability, his bow ties, his three packs of Chesterfields a day, and he seemed to be doing well.

Chapter 8

We were sitting at the windows of my parents' bedroom, my Aunt Rose, my mother, and myself. My mother had my little brother on her lap. It was an overcast Saturday afternoon. It had drizzled earlier in the day.

"Aren't you glad you live here?" my mother said to Rose. "We know everyone in the neighborhood here."

"I'm not glad I live anywhere."

"Rose! Don't talk that way."

"Why was I born anyhow? That's what I'd like to know."

"Marty will be back. He's on the road selling. He's a man. He's got to make a living."

"He should've been back last week . . . He probably *is* back."

"Now don't get upset. He'll call when he gets home. You're lucky you have a man that works hard."

"I don't 'have' anyone."

"Don't say that. You're a lucky girl. You've got a nice family like us . . . And look where you live. You know Sadie Schmoller? She calls herself Sally now. She lives with her husband, Frank what's-his-name, over near the Concourse."

"Frank Stein. Frank N. Stein."

"No, seriously," my mother said, laughing, "Sadie who went to high school with me. She lives on 170th Street and she thinks she's hot stuff because she lives near two subways. I bumped into her the other day at The Griddle. Danny and I went in to have pancakes for lunch. You should have heard her. Putting on airs about her new location. Well, I agreed with her to her face." She turned to me. "It's always best to agree with people. That's why I'm popular. They like me." Then to my aunt, "But underneath I thought to myself, 'Big deal! Who wants to live near two subways?' I wouldn't live there if you paid me. Sure, it's convenient if you work, like she does, but I've got better things to do." She picked my brother up and set him on the floor. Straightened his new outfit, one of the four she bought him when we met Sadie. "I've got my kids to take care of. This little *vonce* and Danny, the smartest kid in the world." She brushed my hair out of my eyes. I watched the traffic lights change at the corner. Red and green. Our neighborhood wasn't wealthy enough to have orange.

"No," my mother said, "I don't envy Sadie. I wouldn't work if you paid me. Not with two fine boys like these. Look at the mouth on Herbie, with Fanny working, and you'll see what I mean. You won't catch my Danny with a mouth like that. Danny doesn't have a mean bone in his body. He takes after us . . . the Farbers."

"Why was I born?" my aunt said.

"You know what? Why don't you get a job? It'll make you feel better."

Rose didn't answer. My mother said to me, "I used to work in the Woolworths. I could sell anything. Anything they couldn't move, they would give to me. I had my own little booth at the front of the store. At Easter they would dress me as a bunny and if they had candy there for six months they couldn't move, they'd give it to me and I'd sell it. Whatever they had. At Thanksgiving they would dress me up as a turkey. Any *chozzerai* in the store I could move. And you know why? Because I love people. That's why they'll buy anything from me. Because people can sense it. People know I love them when they first meet me. Boy, were they sorry when I left to get married. I go in the store now, they've got crap piled up to the ceiling. And Mr. Weineke, he's still the manager, he always says to me, 'I wish you were still here, Ceil. You could move this *dreck* in a second.' I think he had a crush on me, Mr. Weineke. Maybe I should have married him. But I'd never go back to work there. And he knows it. Not when I'm happily married and the mother of two fine boys."

She moved the hair out of my eyes again, but it hadn't really been in my eyes.

"That's why I like our location," my mother continued. "We've got two shopping neighborhoods to choose from. I thought of that, but I didn't say it to Sadie. I didn't want to make her jealous. I figured telling her Sid bought a liquor store when her husband owns a lousy toy store was enough. She got the point. She was burning up, I could tell. But she had to congratulate me." My mother began to laugh. "Oh, listen, Rose, you know what I did? I called her Sadie. I pretended I didn't know she calls herself Sally now. She can't fool me. I knew her when. 'Hi, Sadie,' I said, right out loud in The Griddle. I played dumb. Yeah. Dumb. That's a good one. Dumb like a fox."

"I wish I was never born," my aunt said, abstractedly, as she began to eat a second package of Chuckles sugarcoated candies.

"Listen to her, if you couldn't see her, you wouldn't know she was the beauty of the family."

"Yeah, the beauty."

"You are." My mother turned to me. "When she was little you should've seen her . . . She was five years younger than me."

"Now I'm five years older," my aunt said, lighting up a Raleigh cigarette.

"No . . . No kidding . . . She was the beauty."

"Mommy, who's older, you or Uncle Bernie?"

"Oh, Bernie is. By far. Over two years older . . . Almost three . . ."

My mother was the beauty of the family and Rose was the baby, and they both knew this, but Rose appreciated my mother's attempt to build up her confidence. My mother always did try to say things to people that would make them feel good and that was one of the reasons she was widely liked in our neighborhood.

"Look at your aunt, Danny. Isn't she pretty?"

I nodded yes. My aunt smiled. And Rose *was* pretty, with her dark, rich hair and her smooth skin. Her teeth, though, were another story.

My Aunt Rose wouldn't go to the dentist. She wouldn't deal with pain. Her teeth were beginning to yellow and rot. Two on the upper left were visibly missing.

I *had* to go to the dentist. My father's dentist. Dr. Milton. I had to go regularly with my father. And how did he know that Dr. Milton was a good dentist? Simple. Dr. Milton didn't believe in drugs or in any new-fangled painless dentistry. He believed pain was only mental. So Dr. Milton had to be a good dentist because he hurt people.

My father thought a measured amount of pain was cleansing. When I fell down and scraped my knee my father put iodine on the wound. Not mercurochrome.

"Please, Daddy, can't you use mercurochrome? Iodine hurts."

"I know it hurts, goddamn it. It's supposed to hurt. It's burning out the germs."

When he washed my hair, he had to use Tincture of Green Soap which burned my eyes. I didn't bother to remonstrate after a while. I knew the answer. "It's burning the dirt away. The others don't hurt because they don't do anything."

And after all, wasn't Dr. Milton *his* dentist, too? And didn't my father use iodine and Tincture of Green Soap on himself? It wasn't as if he were saying one thing and doing another.

And perhaps you could even extend this to my frequent beatings at his hands. Perhaps you could say he only beat me up because he beat himself up as well. Perhaps not. He certainly did work hard during this period. He worked six days a week at his store. Then, on Sundays, he would look after the buildings, doing the books and arguing with the tenants. In the mornings, on days when he worked the late shift at the store, he would see to calling the plumber, going to court, meeting with the accountant, and so on.

But he generally found enough time to beat me up. Especially when he worked the early shift. I spent some of the longest afternoons in my life waiting for him to come home after my mother had called him and told him I'd been bad. I would often beg my mother, "Mommy, please, you hit me. Hit me, please." But my mother was too kindhearted to hit me, so she had to call my father. And I had to wait.

Now there are different ways to hit a kid. My grandfather was not adverse to giving me a swat now and then, but his swats were just that, a simple smack, *Bang*, on the ear, a brief cry, and all was forgotten. You felt he had somehow intuited the rules for effective punishment which I later learned were enunciated by Cesare Beccaria in the eighteenth century (swift, certain, fitting the crime).

But my father. Well. I'd be sitting in my room, waiting, when the front door of our apartment would fly open, banging against the wall, "Where is he? Where is that rotten kid?" He would come stalking me with a horrible expression on his face that, amazingly, wasn't put on for effect. It really was a world class, adult, full-fledged, grimace, directed toward this little kid who was cowering in his room. Then he would burst upon me, pulling his belt out of his pants in one swoop, shouting insanely and wildly flailing, raining blows upon me as I begged for mercy until my mother would step in, screaming, "Sid! Sid, are you crazy! Not on his head, Sid." But by then he was so far gone, so out of his mind, that he would hit her with the belt, too, as she stepped between us, and I'd scream, "Daddy, Daddy, I'm sorry," and my mother would scream, "Sid, enough! Enough already! Are you crazy?" until he would finally come to his senses and would slump into the other room, into the world of debts and work and shoulder-wearying obligations of varying degrees of reality and imagination, and my mother would hold me as I sobbed, and she would say, "My sweet baby . . . He's crazy . . . A madman . . . He's crazy . . . Let me go make you a sandwich before your dinner . . . You'll feel better . . ." And my brother would be crying, too, even though he hadn't been hit, and I would lie there sobbing, more at the knowledge than the pain, the knowledge that the gruesome play in which I had been trapped so often would have another performance the next time I made my mother angry, and at the disappointment I felt in my mother for calling him, and in my father for having beaten me, and for allowing such unnecessary ugliness to possess his face when he did it, ugliness I didn't want to see on him, and didn't want him to yield to.

Chapter 9

The more my father beat me up, the more I liked it when he would pick on the wrong person and get beat up himself.

One Sunday morning when I was about ten years old, my mother said, "Come on, Sid. Let's get out. Let's go to the Automat and take the kids to the park."

My father resisted but my mother won out. I loved those afternoons in Van Courtlandt Park. My father only took us there a few times, but I cherished the opportunity to be with my family and to shag fly balls with my brother. And my father seemed to hit the ball so far. I was proud of him. When the men on the block got a permit to play their annual game at McCombs Dam Park, my father was relegated to the role of pinch hitter. But in Van Courtlandt Park, with no pitcher, just fungoing the ball out to us by himself, he shone in my eyes.

At the Automat we got our usual meals of hot vegetables and hamburgers. My father, as always, ordered creamed corn and "red beets." Then we drove up Broadway toward 242nd Street. My father was listening to the Yankee game and he was a mite cheerful. He'd bet on the Yankees for twenty bucks against the Washington Senators and Charlie (King Kong) Keller had homered to give the Yanks a 1-0 lead, but as we got up near Baker Field, Mickey Vernon, the Washington first baseman, hit a three run double off Bill Bevins and suddenly it was 3-1 Senators. My father shouted, "Mickey Vernon! Mickey Vernon goddamn it! That son of a bitch always beats the

Yankees."

My mother didn't pay any attention to him. She was looking at the clothes the women on the streets were wearing. She didn't know who Mickey Vernon was and she didn't care. She didn't even know Eddie Yost from Eddie Joost. Nor did she know that my father had bet the Yankees that day.

But I knew. And I saw him heating up as "that son of a bitch" Mickey Vernon began to spoil his Sunday. It was the one day on which he had a lean chance of peace and satisfaction before returning to the wars on Monday for his seventy-five-hour workweek with his "partner" and his "competitor" and the various other mythological figures who haunted that part of his life which we didn't see, that part of his life which was not haunted by "the tenants."

"That's a nice hat. That blue one," my mother said. "You haven't bought me a hat in a long time." When my father pretended not to hear, she added, "In fact, we haven't shopped for clothes for the whole family."

"Didn't we drive down to the Lower East Side two weeks ago?"

"For *underwear*. I'm not talking underwear. I mean fall outfits. For the boys and myself. We should go up to Fordham next week when you're off at night. The boys'll need new suits for your Cousin Flo's wedding in Brooklyn. And I'll need a new dress . . ."

"I just bought you a new dress. Two months ago. It cost me sixty bucks. I bought you a goddamn *gown*."

"But I wore that already. To Phil's son's *bar mitzvah*. We have to go to Fordham. To get the boys suits at Howard Clothes."

"The boys *have* suits."

"They're outgrowing them."

"That goddamn Danny. I spend half my money on shoes for him."

"No, you don't."

"Can I get shoes on 170th Street?" I said. "I like to look in the X-ray machine where you can see your toes through your shoes."

"You don't *need* shoes, goddamn it," my father said.

I realized I had better be quiet. I didn't want to attract the metal of my father's anger away from the magnet that was already tugging at him that day—Mickey Vernon.

"No, you don't need shoes right now, Danny. Your father's right." My father breathed easier. "But you and your brother will need new suits . . ."

My father tightened his grip on the steering wheel. He began to recite his daily litany as we all turned away and looked out of the windows.

"You know I have a fourteen-hundred-dollar mortgage due on the thirteenth, and my brother Sol in Brooklyn I owe him five hundred bucks, and he won't let me rest in peace, but the store only took in twenty-eight hundred sixty-seven bucks last week and we got twelve hundred in bills and only one hundred fifty seven in the bank, and we owe Miller over at the bank four hundred . . ."

And on and on he continued in his lament of dollar lack, his hands clinging to the steering wheel as if it were a life preserver, the only thing keeping him afloat in a sea of debts and notes and mortgages, until suddenly his sad rant, the single theme with variations which he repeated to himself day after day, his Shakespearean monologue in the theater of money, suddenly his compounded aria of dollar-lament and debtor-woe was interrupted by a roar on the radio. Mel Allen's voice said excitedly in his warm Alabama accent which so charmed the people of The Bronx, "Well, you heard it, folks, Mickey Vernon with a scintillating stab speared that line drive off the bat of Tommy Henrich stranding Jerry Coleman on third and Scooter Rizzuto on second to get the Senators out of the inning once again . . . Fans, when you're thirsty, think of the three rings . . . Purity, body, and flavor . . . And ask the man for Ballantine. Ballantine beer . . ."

My father reached over and clicked off the radio.

"I saw the nicest peach-colored blouse at Wertheimer's the other day," my mother said, innocently enjoying the ride as we approached the end of the El line and the beginning of Van Courtlandt Park. My father sat there getting that little sly look on his face, just nodding his head without really listening to my mother, nodding slightly, yes, yes, as, yes, the synapses in his brain began to open out into a metaphysical, an almost Manichean, dimension, as, yes, the sparks began to sing and shift inside his head and the sweet electrical smell was unmistakable as my father began to sink into full acceptance, once more, of the fact that he was up against larger forces here than notes and mortgages. He was up against much more fearful and unyielding foes than Abe the bookie and the Washington Senators. Yes, my father saw again what he had seen so many times before, and what it seemed he was forced to see each day, my father saw what he had seen when his father died and he was just a boy on the Lower East Side, he saw what he had seen when the Italian kids would come from Mott Street to beat the hell out of him, he saw what he had seen when he had gotten stuck with a rotten kid like me who wore his shoes out too soon, he saw what he had seen when he came to be nineteen years old and ready to make his mark on the world and the stock market crashed . . . yes, my father saw once again that it was the devil himself he was contending with, nothing less, and there was no way, no way he was going to win, because the devil took all these different forms, and you couldn't choke them all: like today, my father's one day of rest, the devil had appeared to taunt him again and again: he appeared as Ceil, his spendthrift wife, he appeared as Danny, his expensive kid, and he had even appeared as Mickey Vernon. Yes, even seemingly innocent Mickey Vernon, the slim first baseman who was apparently just going about his business, was, in some arcane way, on some other, hieratic dimension, working to thwart my father's hopes and plans, to damage him in a way which would prevent him from following his hard work and worry and concern to a decent American life of wealth and ease and security and happiness, and all that was left for my father to do in the face of the awesome magnitude of his foe, the sole joy left to him, was to catch the devil when he was embodied in a single human being and to choke, choke, choke him . . .

The little smile on my father's face was actually the green leer of incipient revenge.

But there, on our right, as we came alongside the park, was a parking space. Could you believe it? A parking space sitting right there like a wounded duck on the ground next to a starving man, the one thing that had gone right all day. My father carefully pulled up beside it, passed it, stopped, put the car in reverse, looked into the rear view mirror, and watched the guy in the car behind us nose into the space and steal it from him.

In one swoop, my father flew out of the door and was on the man, reaching through his window, strangling him with both hands as if he were ringing out a wet towel. And my mother was out on the street, pulling at my father, "Sid! Sid!" in a terrified frenzy, and the stranglee's wife was out and around the car and hitting at my father with her little fists. But my father kept on . . . twisting . . . until the man managed to get his feet up against the door and to push the door open in one quick thrust that sent both my mother and my father to the ground on their backs, my father on top of my mother. The man leaped out. He was *big*. Immediately he was on top of my father as my mother scrambled away, her light blue Sunday suit smeared with gutter grime. The man punched my father in the face, breaking my father's glasses and cutting his nose, and an entire Italian softball team with green and gold jerseys saying "Fontanella's" broadly across the chest came running over to break it up because they saw women were somehow involved. The big guy landed an overhand right to the top of my father's head, and they continued to grapple with each other, rolling over and over on the ground, before the Italians succeeded in pulling them apart. My father felt with his right hand for the blood he knew was dripping from his cut nose. He barked out his case to this Italian jury, "He stole my place," and then he and the guy he had choked struggled to get at each other once again. The guy's wife tried to calm him down as my mother sat on the curb, her legs crossed, disoriented, crying. Two of the softball players attempted to comfort her. I sat in the back of my father's car, watching it all through the rear window, my little heart pumping excitement into my veins, fearful, overstimulated, and filled with slightly guilty glee.

Chapter *10*

When I first began to venture out into the world alone, I was limited by the fact that I wasn't allowed to cross the street. Then I advanced to the next stage—I was allowed to ask an adult to "cross me." When I was finally able to cross streets by myself, I moved into a wider and surprisingly chaotic and violent world. It seemed that each block was the turf of a gang of kids led by a lunatic.

On Plimpton Avenue, behind our house, there was a group led by a madman named Philbert Pauley. Philbert was about two years older than me. He was very big and very strong and very stupid. Fortunately he was not a serious threat to kids my age because the kids he organized were younger than I was, so all he could do was appear around the corner in a mad charge with his followers and terrorize kids my brother's age. Pauley had some medieval notions about the world. As he got older, he picked up certain words like "forsooth" and "swain" and "varlet" which he would spew forth as he would charge down the block with his followers, terrifying succeeding generations of little kids.

He was always somewhat disquieting, this Pauley, and when he got to be six feet two and continued this strange behavior he became a living legend among those who lived in our part of The Bronx. He was unnerving in the way a big dog is when he foams at the mouth on a hot day. You could usually coax Pauley off the block, however, by saying, in a western movie American Indian dialect: "You Plimptons brave. You return to your territory now. You have once again upheld

the Plimpton honor and have gained the Nelsons' undying respect."
If you kept a straight face, he would generally leave and not scare
your little brother for a while.

One block in the other direction, on Shakespeare Avenue, there
was crazy Mickey O'Halloran and the Shakespeare Tong. Apparently
Mickey had heard somewhere about Chinese gangs called "Tongs,"
so he changed the name of his gang from merely, "The Shakespeares,"
to "The Shakespeare Tong." He had each kid steal a large, two-pronged
fork from his mother's kitchen, the kind of fork you'd use to reach
into a fire to spear a baked potato. He thought these were "tongs."
Every now and then he'd lead a large gang of kids around the corner
and they would invade our block, making "Chinese" faces while emit-
ting crazed piercing cries. They would chase us down the street brandishing their "tongs" as we yelled, "Maaaa! Help!" and scattered in
terror.

On the next block south on our own street, there was a group
of Jewish lunatics led by a guy named Ronnie Osterman. Everyone
called him "Ronoso." These dementos appeared on our block every
once in a while in a mad charge directly down the center of the street—
nothing subtle, just a straight-ahead barbarian invasion. They tore
up whatever and whomever they could get their hands on until various
mothers (or my Uncle Lenny), hearing their deranged cries, ran
downstairs and drove them off.

We didn't go north on Nelson Avenue very often because of a
moron named Willie "Hammerhead" Morgan. Willie was called
"Hammerhead" because his head seemed unnaturally foreshortened
at the top. He had virtually no forehead and his widely set, dead eyes
gave him the cruel, implacable aspect of a hammerhead shark. Only
his teeth seemed alive.

Hammerhead was two years older than I but was a grade behind
me in school. He was one of the few Catholics whose parents didn't
send their kids to The Sacred Heart School. He was a rough number
and we all tried to steer clear of him. There was no way, however,
to avoid running into him once in a while at the movies.

Fifteen movie theaters were within walking distance or a short
bus ride from our neighborhood. Each presented different dangers.

The theaters themselves were packed with kids on Saturday afternoons, barely kept in control by middle-aged women in white suits

called "Matrons."

No one wanted to get thrown out of a theater into the bright street because if you did, you had to make it home alone, without your friends, through the turf of jealous kids who didn't like having you in their neighborhood. The most dangerous theater was the Ogden, because you had to climb down some boulders in an empty lot to get home. The lot was the territory of the kids who would later become "The Ikes." If they sprung up from behind the rocks and nabbed you they would torture you until they tired of it.

The most dangerous theater on the inside was the Zenith which had a huge fire ax on the wall. No one thought anything about this object until one afternoon, after we had thoroughly enjoyed watching a Tarzan movie in which Cheetah outsmarted the Nazis, Hammerhead Morgan *threw* the fire ax at my Cousin Herbie.

I had seen dozens of children run onto the stage of Loew's 167th Street theater and tear down the curtains after a particularly hilarious Abbot and Costello movie, but somehow Hammerhead Morgan advanced us one giant step beyond childhood tortures in empty lots. The sound of that big ax as it slapped against the wall and bonged to the floor at Herbie's feet reverberated in my imagination for many years to come.

Chapter 11

At Christmas we had no tree in our apartment. We did have a *menorah*. My grandmother would come in every day to supervise the lighting of the Hanukkah candles.

My grandmother and I had made our peace. She'd stopped calling me *schmutz*, and had earned my affection and respect. One day, when she was making lunch for me, she told me how to say "bread" in Russian, German, Yiddish, and Polish.

"You speak all those languages, Grandma?"

She nodded yes, somewhat bashfully at my astonishment. To my eyes a new aspect had been revealed of this woman who couldn't read or write English, but who kept the Jewish and family traditions alive and who, even though she was the landlord's wife, never lorded it over anyone. She was universally liked (i.e., liked by everyone on our block and the next block on Nelson Avenue—which amounted to almost 1500 people). She always dressed simply. I loved the way the Hanukkah candles lit up her strawberry-gold hair.

My grandfather continued to live in semi-retirement, respected, looking after his buildings with the help of my father, meeting with his old friends from the bakers' union for a glass of tea, taking me to Orchard Beach occasionally, pursuing an active role in the affairs of his little storefront synagogue, and still not riding the trolleys on the Sabbath. Or, I should say, not riding the buses, because that great general who won World War Two, General Motors, had convinced the people of The Bronx, along with the people of Los Angeles and many other American cities, to tear up the tracks of their already built, efficient, smog-free, trolley systems and to replace them with gasoline-burning, internal combustion-engined buses. Buses built by the old general himself.

So our lovely pale-yellow trolleys, with removable windows replaced by iron screens on hot summer days, our rumbly beloved trolleys, disappeared from the hilly streets of the West Bronx forever.

And this change was generally approved of. Everyone was buying a car or planning to buy one, and it was felt that the greater mobility of buses would speed traffic along. As my father said once, after a discussion of this matter, "Let me tell you so you'll understand. A trolley has to run on tracks. That's the main difference. A trolley can't run off its tracks. That's why a bus is superior." And my mother glowed at his wise demeanor in summing up this argument.

My father was doing well, now that he owned a liquor store. He was getting a sense of accomplishment about this advancement in his life, and a sense of authority as he earned people's jealousy and respect. It was about this time that he began to stay out of discussions until the end and then to summarize them with a final remark prefaced by, "Let me tell you so you'll understand."

For example, one night there was a discussion of the results of the 1948 presidential election over coffee and cake with several aunts and uncles and some of my mother's adult cousins who also lived in our building. This colloquy made my father nervous. "I never talk politics or religion. It's no way to run a business." Since he wasn't running a business, but was sitting at home talking with his relatives, I couldn't see how this applied, but when he couldn't re-direct the conversation he took his patriarchal role of the reasonable judge.

He gave everyone a chance to say his or her piece about Dewey or Truman, and then, when all had been given a fair chance to present arguments, he told them "the truth" with a finality that ended the discussion: "Now, let me tell you so you'll understand. This election was a big surprise. Everyone expected Dewey to win. But Truman won. And you know why? You know why Truman won? I'll tell you why so you'll understand. Truman was more popular than Dewey. You see, more people wanted Truman than Dewey. So Truman won."

This wonderfully simple statement brought a satisfied smile to his face and earned him the respect of the aunts and uncles. After all, my father now owned half a liquor store and half an apartment house. He had a four-room apartment, a pretty wife, and two kids. Granted, he didn't live in an elevator building, but he was young and who could doubt that there was a good chance that someday he *would* live in an elevator building? So he must have known "the truth." And all the others, my Cousin Jonah who was shot in the leg in the war and who worked in a grocery store, my Uncle Albee who drove a taxi, my father's sisters and mother's cousins, they wanted to find the truth too, and to reach that second Garden of Eden—the land of financial security.

My Uncle Bernie, of course, was not so impressed with either my father's brilliant insights or his style. He laughed when my father spoke *ex cathedra* and would often get my Aunt Rose laughing, too.

My father did not speak with final authority, however, when our cousin, Saul Pischkin, was around. Saul not only owned his own *house* in Jersey, he had *silent light switches* in his house. Yes, when you turned on a light, did it go "click"? Not in Saul's house. Silent as a lovely mid-winter snowfall in Paramus. "You don't hear nothing and, poof, like magic, the light is on."

"Suppose someone is sleeping," my mother said. "I'll give you a for instance. Say Saul falls asleep on his lounge chair that reclines backwards if you want in the living room when he's home from work and he's reading his *Journal American*. And Frieda wants to put the light out for him. So he'll enjoy his rest. He works hard all day. Doesn't he deserve a little rest in the evening after he's had his *latkes* and applesauce? Well, this is when Frieda tiptoes into the room and switches off the light. And is there a click? Is there a single sound to wake up her man? Not one. Not one sound. And there he sleeps, peacefully as you could ask for."

"You see the beauty of it?" my father said. "You see the beauty of it?"

"A light that goes on without a sound!" my Uncle Lenny said, considering this with fundamental wonder. "Go figure baseball. A light without a sound."

"It's an idea whose time has come," my father said.

My Uncle Lenny often said, "Go figure baseball." In his good-natured way, he seemed impressed and amazed by everyone and everything in The Bronx. He did not tell jokes himself, but he was the kind of person everyone told jokes to. He seemed continually grateful and surprised to be living in a neighborhood with so many respectable and talented people.

We didn't know much about his background except for the stories he regaled us with about his adventures as a poor teenager on the Lower East Side, and to see him there, in front of the building, in his tee-shirt with his tattoos showing and his head as bald as the man on the Joyvah Halvah package, telling stories—well, we kids loved it.

The adults liked Lenny, too. When he worked for Manny at the luncheonette, all the truck drivers would stop in to say hello when they delivered the afternoon newspapers. Art, the man who drove the crimson *New York Sun* truck would say, "I bet the Giants again. So listen, this afternoon, up at Braves Field, we got Dave Koslo pitching and I got twenty bucks down on the Giants and we're ahead one to nothing in the ninth. So they let Johnny Sain, the pitcher, hit for himself with two men on and he doubles in two runs and I'm out twenty bucks. Can you believe it?"

"They let the pitcher hit for himself in the last of the ninth?" Lenny said, with his usual expression of amazement. "And he hit a double?" He smiled. "Go figure baseball," he said. "Go figure baseball."

He continued to work irregularly ("Where do they get their money?" my father still said), but when he did work, he was reliable and trustworthy. In fact, he once received a medal from the local police for helping Tiny Nizell, a 400-pound cab driver, capture a gunman who had held up the Daitch Dairy on Eddie L. Grant Highway.

I was in my house at the time when I heard what I thought were firecrackers. But it was not the right time of year for firecrackers, which were sold at a "secret" store on Gun Hill Road known only to half The Bronx. At the next moment, my brother and my friend, Fat Heshie Jankowitz, who, like myself, was ten years old, ran into the house. They were both pale as farina. Heshie dashed straight into the bathroom and locked the door.

What had happened was that when a man held up the cashier at Daitch's, an off-duty policeman, Whitey Grogan, was moonlighting there, unloading cartons of groceries onto the shelves. Grogan got the brilliant idea that he could be a hero. He pulled out his service revolver and began to shoot it out with the robber right in the store as everyone fell to the floor and rolled for cover while summoning Jehova, Jesus, or the God of their choice for assistance.

The robber ran from the store, Grogan still firing at him, his bullets breaking windows not only in Daitch's itself, but all the way across Eddie L. Grant Highway in Nat's Fishmarket. Grogan chased him around the corner to Nelson Avenue across the street from our house. They took cover behind parked cars as they proceeded up the block, at one point firing at each other right next to my brother and Fat Heshie who were playing hit the penny with a Spaldeen on the sidewalk. Everyone scattered into doorways. Uncle Lenny, who had been standing in front of Max the barber's, joined Grogan in the chase, which finally wound up in the vacant lot on the next block. The robber ran out of bullets and surrendered. But just as Uncle Lenny and Tiny Nizell arrived on the scene, the robber proceeded to beat Grogan over the head with his gun butt. Grogan whacked the robber's head with his own gun, but the robber had the element of surprise. At the third whack Grogan went down, but here my uncle and Tiny Nizell *tackled* the gunman and brought *him* down. When the clerks from Daitch's arrived to help, the fight had gone out of the robber, now breathless, friendless, and bulletless. Tiny Nizell sat on him until the police came.

We finally convinced Fat Heshie to come out of our bathroom. He emerged shaken and white. He kept repeating, "I could hear them whistle right by my head. The bullets. Jeez, it was just like a movie . . ."

Chapter *12*

Aunt Rose continued to languish in her parents' apartment, unemployed, going to the movies less frequently, seeing Marty occasionally, but most often pining away for him, eating sweets and suffering toothaches.

Uncle Bernie was becoming increasingly restless as assistant to Ida at the record store. Often he went drinking with Marty. They each drove large cars. They looked something like one another, with their sporty clothes and trimmed mustaches. On many Sunday nights, Bernie would come to our house with his family and he would entertain. My mother had bought a new spinet piano which she liked to play from time to time, but mostly she thought it looked good in the living room and gave Bernie a chance to perform. Bernie would play on the black keys, rolling octaves as he sang, "For it was Mary, Mary," and the other old songs he and the aunts and uncles loved.

My father was acting less erratically when I was eight and nine. Once he even got some free tickets from a liquor salesman and took me to a football game. The time he really came through was the evening I broke my arm. It happened just after dinner when I was eight years old. Herbie was chasing me up the block, shooting at me with a water gun. Shooting back at him over my shoulder, I spun blindly into the alley of our building. When I turned forward, I saw I was about to run into Stefan Pulaski, the super, and Hymie Herman, a Hebrew teacher who lived in our building. Hymie was a man about my mother's age, but he dressed like he had just come out of the *shtetl*, and he was poor. My mother kept her distance from him. He and Stefan were walking up the alley together. To avoid running into them I put on the brakes, fell forward, and jammed my left arm into the ground, rigidly, trying to break my fall but fracturing my arm instead.

Hymie helped me up and everyone assumed I was merely shaken up, but the odd feeling in my arm wouldn't go away. My father suspected what it was, walked with me to Dr. Stern's office, politely asked the people in the waiting room if he could take me in ahead of them, and then drove me to Harlem to the Hospital For Joint Disease. I was afraid to stay overnight so they set my arm without anesthesia. My mother later told me that my father had wept in the hallway as he heard my screams to him for help, and that one nurse had to stay with him to keep him from responding to my cries.

My mother spoke often about that evening. "One thing I don't understand, Danny. I can understand that Hymie would push you down and break your arm, after all, maybe he didn't mean to push you that hard . . ."

"Hymie didn't push me at all, Ma . . ."

". . . but I just don't see why you should lie to protect him."

"I'm not lying. He didn't push me, Ma. I fell. I was trying not to run into him."

"Imagine . . . A grown man pushing a little boy down! Who ever heard of such a thing?"

"*Ma!* Ask Stefan the super. He'll tell you. I just *fell.*"

"And even if he didn't mean to push you that hard, look at the result."

"*Ma . . . Ask Stefan . . .*"

"And why you protect Hymie, a grown man who broke your arm, I just don't understand."

Chapter 13

1949 was a frustrating year for America. The Russians detonated an atomic bomb well before it had been expected and China fell to the Communists.

It was a disastrous year for our family. In the fall, suddenly and without warning, my grandfather died.

I knew something was wrong when I was awakened for school by a roomful of whispering women. My Aunt Fanny was there, and Aunt Bessie, and Aunt Hilda, and even Mrs. Weiss, who stuttered and had babysat for me often when I was younger.

"What's up?" I said, sleepily.

"Your grandfather passed away last night, Danny," my Aunt Bessie said. "Just go to school. It'll be all right."

But it wasn't all right, although I did feel a certain distinguishing importance, being the grandson of someone who had "passed away." In the living room people were talking quietly, centered around my mother who was slumped on a chair, red-eyed, weeping pitifully.

The old helmsman was gone and the family ship began to maunder in woe.

My father nervously smoked one Chesterfield after another, looking as Harry Truman must have looked when F.D.R. died and Harry said he felt like a load of hay had fallen on him. My father was slowly trying to come to terms with the fact that he would no longer have my grandfather to rely on, to borrow money from, to ask advice of . . . and that he was going to have to manage several buildings worth thousands of dollars (with mortgages also worth thousands of dollars). With my grandmother collapsed he was now effectively partners with Uncle Bernie, Aunt Rose, and my mother.

And my grandmother's collapse turned out to be more than ephemeral. She never recovered. The family had to hire a live-in nurse to take care of her, at great expense, and even though sometimes they brought her out at a family gathering in our apartment, when, say, my Uncle Bernie would show up with his ukelele and play, "If you knew ukelele baby," she would just sit there in a gloomy, confused, silence. She seemed to atrophy. She became more helpless as time went on and she died about a year later. She had become so reliant on my grandfather's great strength that she had forgotten her own.

My grandfather's death was the beginning of a difficult period for all of us. The center hadn't held. Things fell apart.

My Uncle Bernie began to drink heavily. My Aunt Rose stayed in the house with her sick mother and the nurse, moping about, longing for Marty. My father began to lose his hair more quickly and to stoop when he stood as if he were supporting the whole building and the entire family on his shoulders.

The tenants, of course, were nice enough to come to the door to remind him of all the promises my grandfather had made to them, promises real and imagined, about paint jobs and new bathroom fixtures and the next four-room apartment. They also came to him with their complaints about each other, as if he were, in some way, really the lord of the land, there not only to take their rent, but to arbitrate their disputes in return.

"Mr. Schwartz, please," old Mrs. Lurie said, "it's Hafter up in 4B. He walks around heavy on my ceiling. On purpose, Mr. Schwartz."

"I told him, Mrs. Lurie. I told him twenty times. What do you want me to do? He's got to walk. He can't fly, Mrs. Lurie."

"I'm a helpless woman, Mr. Schwartz. If Mr. Farber, he should only rest in peace, were alive, he would do something . . ."

"OK, OK, I'll talk to him . . ."

Then, a week later, Hafter would come down. "Mr. Schwartz, please, you've got to do something. I'm living over a madwoman. Every night now, she stays home and she has a broom and she bangs up on the ceiling with a broomstick."

"She *what?*"

"She must be on a chair or something. Every evening. Bang, Bang, Bang. Right under my feet. I'm a working man, Mr. Schwartz. I gotta relax at night. How can I live with her banging under my feet?"

Or periodically, there'd be yelling in the hall and a loud crash and my mother would scream, and I would know one of the tenants had pushed my father down the stairs.

"Sid!" my mother would implore, as he lay there disoriented on the floor and she smoothed his hair looking for lumps on his head. "Sid, how *could* you do that? You can't fight with Shimkas. He's a sheet-metal worker. He works with his hands."

"I'll kill him," my father would say, quietly, jerking his head from side to side like a boxer trying to shake off a punch as he sat up. "I'll kill the son of a bitch."

"You can't choke the tenants, Sid. Are you crazy? My father never choked the tenants."

But my father would sit there, eyes glazed, not listening to her, planning his revenge.

Meanwhile, we were sending hourly messages regarding the condition of my grandmother on the people's telegraph which, to the uninitiated, would appear to be a mere dumbwaiter for the super to collect the garbage. But to those in the know, it was actually a secret message system. You "called" someone by beating on the riser steam-pipes which ran straight up from the basement through all the apartments in a line. Thus if we, in apartment 1I, wanted to call my Aunt Fanny in apartment 3I, we would hit the steam pipe three times with a heavy metal spoon or the back of a knife, and then open the dumb-waiter and look up. There, on the third floor up the shaft, my aunt's head would appear, and we could hold a conversation. If we hit the pipe four times, my Aunt Hilda on the fourth floor would appear.

Part of the delight in using this message system derived from the fact that it seemed as if somehow you were getting away with something since you saved a nickle on a phone call. It seemed that if the authorities had found out about this, AT&T would have taken over our dumb-waiters and charged us for using them.

As for myself, I was continuing to get A's in school and S's in "Works and plays well with others" on my report cards. I was what you could call "highly motivated." Every day I brought twenty sharpened pencils to school in my pencil box in case the points on nineteen of them should break. And each year, on the last day of class, my mother would make sure that I washed my hair and wore new clothes so as to make sure I wasn't "left back."

As more stations and shows came on, we all began to watch more television. My Cousin Herbie, who was still my closest friend, continued to complain about his father not having a regular job.

"You're lucky," I said. "Your father's around all the time to play with us. My father's never around."

"Your father loves you. More than you know."

"Your father loves you, too, Herbie."

"Yeah. We don't even have a TV."

But shortly thereafter, my Uncle Lenny went off on a business trip for two weeks and bought them a TV when he returned.

"You see," I said. "You got a TV now."

"Yeah, yeah. At least you got a Philco. What kinda set does my old man get? A Dumont! Who the hell wants to watch a goddamn Dumont?"

But we did watch. Especially the hockey games. Ice hockey was not played in our neighborhood since there were no skating rinks or bodies of water except the Harlem River and it didn't freeze. So it was TV that introduced us to the game. And to the realization that the lobby of our building, large, rectangular, tile-floored, without furniture, with a small set of stairs at each end, was shaped like a hockey rink.

With my grandfather dead, my father busy at work, and Stefan the super drunk every night, it was perfect for night games. We put on roller skates, tied towels around the legs of my brother and his friend Gilbert who were the goalies, and made pucks by purchasing metal rolls of Johnson and Johnson adhesive tape, winding the tape from one roll around the other. We were in business.

Until, of course, the tenants complained to my mother about the noise of the metal wheels on the tiles. My mother then complained to my father who saw that the problem was that I was the instigator and that my mother was too weak to discipline me. So he bought her a cat-o'-nine tails.

Where he got this contraption, I can't imagine. It resembled a policeman's billy club, but with (seven actually) leather straps affixed to the end. The idea was that as soon as she caught us playing hockey,

64

she would run out and begin to whip me with it.

Well, she tried it once, charging out and flailing away, but it was so embarrassing to me to be whipped by my mother with a cat-o'-nine tails in front of my friends, that I charged her and wrestled it away and, in my frenzy, threw it down the sewer.

Strangely enough, there were no repercussions about this from my father. I guess he sensed there was something unkosher about the whole affair. ("Kosher" being defined as "acceptable to the neighbors.")

It was about this time that, of all the rooms in the house, I began to like the bathroom best. It was the only room where I could have some privacy, and, *mirabile dictu*, it even had a lock on the door. If my mother was chasing me, trying to hit me, I could run in there and lock the door and then bargain with her for clemency as my price for coming out. When my father chased me, it was a different story, however. Sometimes, when he was at work, I would practice quickly entering the bathroom and locking the door in one motion and then, when the dreaded chase actually would occur, I could generally make it into the bathroom in time. With my father there was no bargaining.

"Come out of there, pig, before I break your neck."

Silence.

"I said come out of there before I break down the goddamn door."

At this point I would have to slowly open the door and come out and get hit because I knew, in fact, that he would break the door down if he had to and that would get him into an even greater rage. He might actually decide to "re-set" my arm the way he had heard them doing it to me that night at the hospital in Harlem. But I gained precious time, enough for me to come out to an angry father rather than to the madman who had chased me in there.

That "pig" my father had called me had become his usual term for me when he argued with my mother about money. "You're bleeding me dry, Ducky," he would say. "You're bleeding me dry."

"I have to buy the necessities. The kids need things. Danny needs A B C D . . ."

"Danny! All I hear is Danny! That selfish pig!"

Of course there was some justice in my father's claims. For example, at this time, as I prepared to enter junior high school, many of the older kids had formed clubs and bought jackets. Bright, gaudy, satin affairs done up in the club's colors. Well, was this fair? That they should have club jackets just because they belonged to clubs, and that I, the landlord's son, shouldn't, just because I didn't belong to a club? So I talked my mother into buying me a club jacket. And she talked to my father.

"Get him his jacket, Sid. What's the big deal? He'll wear it like any other jacket."

"He's bleeding me dry, the selfish pig . . ."

I was in the next room, listening to the conversation, rooting like mad for the selfish pig, hoping they would give the selfish pig the jacket.

My father took me to Heights Sport over in Manhattan. The man behind the counter said, "Of course I can make you a jacket, young fellah. Where's the rest of your club?"

"I don't have a club."

"I thought you wanted a club jacket?"

"Just make him up a jacket," my father said, trying to indicate to the guy that I was a little touched. The guy caught on.

"What's the colors of this 'club' young man?"

"Blue and gold."

"And the name?"

"The Rovers."

I picked up the jacket two weeks later with my father on a Saturday, and I wore it the following afternoon when my family went to the Automat for lunch. The blue and gold satin shone brightly in the sunlight. As I walked along, I became convinced that everyone was looking at me. I was the only one with a blue and gold jacket.

And then, suddenly, I realized the full implications of "The Rovers" on my back. There *was* a team called The Rovers. A minor-league hockey team which played at Madison Square Garden on Sunday afternoons. They were a farm team of the New York Rangers. Perhaps a few hundred people attended their games, people who couldn't, for the most part, pay the full price to see the Rangers at night.

Yes, I realized the awful truth: All these people I was passing, all these innocent Jewish parents, must have been thinking that I was on the New York Rovers. But I was only eleven years old. And I couldn't even ice-skate.

I knew at that moment there was a simple term for what I had done: Fraud. I had perpetrated a complete and consummate fraud, and all these parents were thinking, "Look at that, that kid is only eleven and he's on the New York Rovers, while my Harry, he's thirteen already, and he hasn't gotten anywhere yet. Wait til I go home and tell him, that bum. Here's a kid two years younger than him and already playing professional hockey."

I looked about, self-consciously. My face turned red. Suppose one of them came up and asked me about the team. What would I say? How would I explain to my parents that my deceit had not been intentional?

"Come along with me, young man," I could almost hear the policeman say.

"I didn't mean it, officer. I swear, I didn't mean it."

"Please officer," my mother would beg, "he says he didn't mean it."

"Hardly likely, ma'm. He admits he doesn't belong to any club. Of all the names in the world, why would he pick "The Rovers" except to perpetrate this dastardly hoax which will only serve to make other Jewish parents think less of their sons in relation to him?"

"Please officer," my mother would be on her knees now, "I've done many favors for the police in my time. I used to work at Woolworths. I'm not unconnected."

"Sorry ma'm. I appreciate your suffering. After all, my mother was a mother too, you know. But I've got to take him on a 607. 'Impersonating a Hockey Player.'"

"The man's right, Ducky," my father would say. "You gotta respect the law. I always say, 'The law deserves respect.'"

When we got home from the Automat, I carefully hung my jacket in my closet and I never wore it again.

Chapter 14

The death of my grandparents brought several changes into our lives. My Aunt Rose was left alone in the big apartment. There were no more large family dinners on Friday nights. No more watching my grandmother light the Sabbath candles while covering her head with a linen napkin; no more getting a dollar from my grandfather when we would play hide the matzo on Passover and I would find it. No more trips on the bus to Orchard Beach, just my grandfather and I, where my grandfather had taught me to swim. No more feelings of surprising pleasure at the way the men and women of my parents' generation would always address him respectfully as *"Mister* Farber" when they met him on the street.

We began, at this time, to drift further from the kosher rules in our household. It had begun with the Chinese food. Before we had purchased our TV we had only eaten Chinese food at the restaurant. But then, my father began to bring it home often on Sunday evenings instead of "Deli."

Once my grandmother was gone, and we had already let unkosher food into our house, how much more unkosher would it be to include an order of delicious Chinese barbecued pork? And once we had barbecued pork on Sunday, why not a BLT or a ham and cheese during the week?

But one dish we never had, in our house or out, was pork chops. Somehow pork chops existed at that node where thousands of years of Biblical proscriptions met the even more divine dictates of modern medical science. If pork chops weren't cooked right, we understood you became afflicted by some weird disease that thank goodness only afflicted the *goyem*. It sounded like "tricky gnosis."

And who knew how to cook pork chops right in the first place? Who was there to teach you except the *goyem*, and if they could believe a Jewish carpenter was GOD, how could you trust them to know the delicate, the intricate, the mysterious subtleties of cooking pork chops? And if they did know this, why was there such a disease as tricky gnosis in the first place?

Chapter *15*

Every neighborhood in New York had a mook and our neighborhood was no different from any other in this respect. Our mook was my Cousin Louie.

Like "genius" and "saint," mook is a word that is hard to define, but you know one if you meet one. For one thing, Louie never cried. In fact, always insecure about money, he would pick up spare change in elementary school by charging people to bang his head on the sidewalk. Everyone would gather round, a guy would give Louie a nickel, and Louie, who was strong as an ox, would agree to submit meekly while the guy banged his head on the concrete. When the guy was finished, Louie would emerge, somewhat shaken, but not crying.

So perhaps this is a hint to what a mook is: A mook is often good-natured, he has a hard head, is strong as a bull, and you can't really hurt him. But there was one other characteristic of a mook which Louie exemplified. A mook is absolutely fearless. This does not arise from some calculated notion of honor or thoughtful courage. No, it is rather as if it never occurs to a mook that a situation might evoke fear. When in danger, a mook will often attack in a blunt, unthinking, bull-like, charge that can terrify an opponent by its very foolhardiness.

For example, once, when he was about fourteen, Louie was attacked by Billy Mulvaney, a tough kid his age, over a questionable "leaner" in a game of pitching baseball cards against a wall. Louie, being a mook, plowed into Billy, slammed him against the wall, threw him on the ground, and then stood over him, straddling him, saying,

"Are you kidding? I eat guys like you for breakfast."

By not continuing his attack on Billy, Louie felt, in his good-hearted way, that he was being generous. Being a mook, he did not realize that verbal assaults can be as damaging as physical assaults, or that his claim that he ate guys like Billy Mulvaney for breakfast would be taken as severely opprobrious and injurious not only to the morale of Billy, but to the entire Mulvaney family. This was unfortunate since Mulvaney's older brother Pat was a first-class lunatic on the verge of being put away for several years for stabbing a girl.

About a week later, Louie was on his way home from Abe the bookie's poolroom. Louie liked to spend time with Abe. He couldn't hang around his own father because my Uncle Bernie spent his nights at the Village Inn with Rose's boyfriend Marty, drinking, telling stories, and flirting with the women. At Abe's Louie ran errands and picked up small change. Louie was fascinated by gambling. Perhaps he hoped to be a bookie himself someday. As Louie proceeded down deserted and dark Nelson Avenue, Pat Mulvaney stepped out of an alley, pulled a knife on him, and said, "I hear you eat guys for breakfast. How'd you like to eat this?"

Well Louie was a mook, but he was not a *total* moron, so before Pat could say another word, Louie burst away and flew down the street, with Pat chasing him, flashing the knife at his back. Louie was a terrific athlete, surprisingly quick for his size, so Pat couldn't catch him. Pat chased him all the way to the Noonan Plaza, past the swan pool in the courtyard, into Louie's building, up two flights of stairs, and to the door of Louie's apartment which Louie slammed in his face and locked.

Now, at this point, an ordinary person would thank his lucky stars he had made it home and go to bed, breathing a sigh of relief. But Louie was not an ordinary person. Louie was a mook. So he ran right past his sister Carol and my Aunt Bessie, into the kitchen, picked up a foot long butcher knife, ran past them again as my aunt screamed, rushed out into the hall, and then *he* chased Pat Mulvaney all the way to *his* house, shouting, "I'll eat you for breakfast, too, you creep."

As I remarked earlier, "mook" is difficult to define precisely, but I hope this example clarifies the matter to some degree.

Chapter 16

As we went through our money from my grandparents' estate, my father seemed to endure a new line on his brow for every dollar we spent. I continued to worry and to eat. I would get especially nervous when my parents quarrelled about money because they generally argued in the kitchen and thus I couldn't eat while they were fighting.

My father always complained about my mother's food bills. According to my mother, she was not like the other mothers on the block—she didn't serve us stale food. Only fresh food. Fresher than any other mother on the block. Nothing was too good for her kids. And by "her kids" we all knew she meant me, because my brother, at this point in his life, hardly ate at all. He was the smallest kid in his class, a "skinny merink" according to my mother. I had become the fattest.

"Can I serve the kids stale cheese, Sid?"

"What stale? What are you talking stale?" He threw open the door of the refrigerator. It was so full, two jars and a package of ham fell on the floor. "Look!" He began to throw packages of cheese on the floor. Swiss, American, Velveeta, Muenster, Swiss Knight, cream cheese, pot cheese . . . all unopened.

"I won't serve my boys stale cheese."

"So get a cheese. But not ten kinds every day."

"Nothing's too good for my Danny."

"And look over here." He went to the garbage from which he

pulled out unopened cans of creamed corn, string beans, baked beans, Campbell's soups. "These cans were never used."

"I bought them three weeks ago. Can I feed Danny crap? You want him to get botulism? Muriel Teitner can feed her kid old canned food, but not my Danny."

My father began to pace around the room, ready to tear his hair out. "My Danny! Danny this and Danny that! That's all I hear around here. He's eating me out of house and home, your Danny." He walked toward their bedroom. "That goddamn kid is eating me out of house and home." He slammed the door behind him, leaving my mother sitting wearily at the kitchen table, her head in her hands.

After a while she rose and wiped her eyes. She picked up the cheese my father had thrown on the floor. She wiped the area around the sink with a paper towel. I walked over to her.

"Ma, can I have a sandwich?"

She lit up. "Sure, Danny, what would you like?"

"Cheese, Ma."

She smiled again. "What kind of cheese, Danny?"

"I don't know. Maybe a combination."

Her face glowed as she opened various packages of cheese and piled slices on Silvercup white bread for me.

In the early fifties my Uncle Bernie bought the record store with his share of the inheritance and we moved across the street to a four-room apartment in the building which my father and my grandfather had bought together. It was an art-deco style, 1930s, white-brick building with twenty-four apartments and an elevator. When my father proudly announced to my Uncle Bernie one night, "Now I live in an elevator building, too, big shot," my uncle, who was drunk, retorted, "Oh, yeah. Does your building have swans? Does it have even one stinkin' swan?," thereby silencing my father once again.

My mother redecorated our new apartment, buying new light fixtures, getting it painted and wallpapered, and purchasing new furniture. This was her dream and she wanted to do it right. Her pride and joy was an individually designed mirror which would almost cover the entire longest wall of the living room. The mirror was over twenty feet long with a heavy glass frame around it. On the frame were hand-painted (mostly in pink) eighteenth-century aristocrats, in couples, the men kissing the ladies' hands, the ladies with parasols.

When we went to the East Bronx to order the mirror the owner of the store, Hal Marx, brought out the artist himself, his brother-in-law, Pierre Fishbein, a French Jew who wore a beret. When my father saw the beret, he got worried. He knew that beret was going to cost him.

"Pierre?" my father said, suspecting a joke.

"I was born in Paris. My family came over here when I was a kid, before the First World War."

"This is exciting," my mother said. "I never met a real artist."

Pierre smiled modestly.

"Er . . . How much do you charge, Mr. Fishbein?" my father said.

"Well, the cost is really secondary. It's the art of it . . . You'll have original art in your house for years and years."

My mother, who believed in "art," was thrilled.

"Yes," my father said, "but tell me Mr. Fishbein, er . . . How much do you charge?"

"Well . . . You pay by the person."

"By the person?"

"Yeah. Each person I paint on there costs fifteen bucks."

"Fifteen bucks a person?"

"Well, you'll need about twenty-eight people on the frame, I guess . . ."

"Gee," my father said. "That's a lot of people."

My mother was delighted, not following the conversation, lost in rapture as she looked at a similar mirror, already completed, leaning against the wall.

"Not really," Fishbein said. "I'll tell you what. I'll give you twenty-eight people for three hundred fifty dollars. And to show you I'm a good sport, I'll throw in fourteen bouquets of flowers between them for a buck a piece."

"That sounds fine, Sid," my mother said, returning to the conversation.

My father was trapped. He didn't really want to pay, but they did have the money and he wasn't accustomed to dealing with artists and not sure what they charged.

"Come on, Sid," my mother implored. "Can't we do it? Think

74

of what everyone in the neighborhood will say when they see it. Real paintings in our living room!"

"I'll tell you what," my father said to Pierre. "You give me thirty people and fifteen flowers for two hundred twenty-five bucks and you got yourself a deal."

"Two hundred forty?" Pierre said.

"You'll absorb the tax?"

"What 'tax'? I'm a simple artist. Tax is for businessmen. What do I know about tax?"

They smiled and shook on it. Then Hal, the owner of the store, said to my mother, "Before you go, why don't you take a look at these French-style lamps over here?" He led her off to another part of the store, saying, "And Pierre can paint the same ladies and gentlemen on them, too, if you like."

As a result of our move across the street, I was obliged to change schools, now going to P.S. 11 with my Cousin Louie instead of to P.S. 104 with my Cousin Herbie. I liked my new school better. Small and old, it had been built right after the Civil War. The principal was a pleasant avuncular man, Mr. Levine, who would come around to the classes from time to time and play the accordion. One day they even brought Tonto, from "The Lone Ranger Show," to our assembly.

I made friends easily because I was a good athlete, but the following year I ran into trouble. I was assigned to the sixth grade class of a teacher named Miss Seltzer who, it later turned out, was a Communist. She was eventually fired for her beliefs. After she had left the neighborhood, everyone always referred to her as "Commie Seltzer."

At the time when I was in her class, the only radical statement I can recall her uttering concerned the United Fruit Company. She urged us to tell our mothers to put their bananas in the refrigerator.

Miss Seltzer possessed one characteristic which frightened the wits out of me, and it wasn't related to her politics. Miss Seltzer looked exactly like my father. She had the same color and texture of hair, the same general physique, the same eyeglasses, and expression on her face—she even had a little mustache similar to my father's.

My life became a nightmare. I had to deal with two Sids now.

The real Sid, at home, plus the false Sid, Miss Seltzer, at school each day. There was no escape. Well, one escape, really. Each morning when I got to school, I would ask to leave the room and head to the toilet where I felt safe. I began to spend more and more time in the bathroom. I loved it in the bathroom. It was so serene there, away from the hustle and bustle of everyday life, from the violence and demands and constraints. Nothing to do but sit there, by yourself, in peace.

Until, one day, Miss Seltzer had had enough of this. In front of the entire class, she forbade me to ever "leave the room" again. Well, I must admit that this biased my attitude toward Communists. I wasn't concerned about what they said about United Fruit. In fact, they might even have been one hundred percent correct about United Fruit, and they might even have been right in their theories about putting bananas in the refrigerator for all I knew, but for several years I believed that Communists were people who would talk your ear off about love of humanity but who wouldn't even let you go to the bathroom when you had to.

So I simply stopped going to school. I preferred to stay at home. Our new apartment had *two* bathrooms. I could choose which one to use according to my mood and stay there at my leisure. When my mother went shopping I had the entire apartment to myself. I could turn on the radio and listen to all the idiotic adults "march around the breakfast table" on "Don McNeil's Breakfast Club." I could read the only books in the house, the Book of Knowledge, which my mother had bought for me. I loved the articles on various far-off cities with pictures of their skylines—Detroit, Cleveland, Pittsburgh, Tacoma . . . distant, romantic places, where people led different and more exciting lives.

At first, my mother was a pushover for my excuses. But as time went on, she began to worry. Finally, after I was taken to three doctors (including a "big man") who could find nothing wrong with me, my father went to my school and confronted Miss Seltzer who was also becoming concerned about my case at this time, lest she be blamed for contributing to the madness of a minor. A compromise was worked out. For the first time in the history of P.S. 11, for the first time since the Civil War no doubt, a kid was to have the run of the school. I, Danny Schwartz, would get the seat nearest the door and I could go to the bathroom anytime I wanted without asking.

So I had my little triumph. And I did go to the bathroom. In spite of the fact that the kids began to call me "the bathroom boy," I went again and again, and when I was down there, by myself, sitting on the toilet seat, I found a certain peace of mind. Let them call me what they would upstairs.

My father, at this time, called me "Fatboy." He used the term as if it were my name. When he came home from work late and we were already in the kitchen, eating dinner, he'd say as he sat down, "Hi, Ducky, Barr, Fatboy," without giving it a second thought.

Then he would join us at dinner. Fried salmon croquettes, spaghetti, canned creamed corn, mashed potatoes, white bread and butter, and Hoffman's strawberry soda, followed by big helpings of home-made chocolate pudding pie piled high with whipped cream.

The fatter I got, the more my father became convinced that it was I who was responsible for his shortages of money. My father had gone further into debt on the purchase of a new maroon Buick which was only slightly larger and more bulky than the battleship Missouri. Of course, having this object of so much value on the street made him even more nervous than usual. He would wake up in the middle of the night and go downstairs to make sure it was still there.

One evening my mother came running into my room. "It's your father, Danny. He's crazy."

"What happened, Ma?"

"Oh, God knows," she sat down on the edge of my bed. "They stole his radio antenna off the car. So he waited til now, when it's dark, and he went out there, walking around The Bronx, looking for a car like ours to steal one back."

Later that night, with my mother still pacing around the apartment, the door flew open and in walked my father with this devilish gleam on his face. He was carrying someone's radio antenna in his hand.

"How *could* you?" my mother said. "You're a liquor store owner. This isn't the Lower East Side. How *could* you?"

"Whaddya mean?" my father said. "They took mine, didn't they?"

They never caught my father so that caper worked out all right for him. Yet it still appeared that the more he moved up in life, the more worried he became, and thus the more he blamed me for eating him out of house and home. Therefore, the more I worried and the more I ate.

One evening, when I was in the sixth grade, I was standing with my Uncle Lenny in front of our new building after dinner. I was playing catch lazily with my Cousin Herbie who stood on the sidewalk across the street. Herbie liked to keep a distance between himself and his father at this time because my uncle had become convinced that it was possible to avoid baldness by toughening your scalp when you were young. So, periodically, on the street, he would grab Herbie by the hair and virtually lift him up by it, growling this big laugh, as Herbie sprayed out a spate of curses and my uncle said to everyone around, "He yells now, but he'll be happy later. He ain't gonna be bald like me when he grows up." Then he would release Herbie who would stumble off, wincing and holding his head and looking at his father as if he were a madman.

On this particular evening, my uncle surprised me by talking about the Boy Scouts. He had never spoken about the Scouts before, but suddenly he couldn't stay off the subject. The Scouts were America and Mom and apple pie all rolled up into one.

A few weeks later I joined the Boy Scouts along with both my cousins and my Uncle Lenny. How my Uncle Lenny was qualified to become an assistant troop leader was not clear to me. Perhaps there was a merit badge for "Preventing Baldness," and he had demonstrated his ability in this area by pulling his son's hair in front of Reuben Norman, the scoutmaster.

But Lenny had the time and the willingness to try. Everyone liked him, and I guess the Boy Scouts in The Bronx needed all the help they could get.

Lenny took us downtown to the Scout store and we bought uniforms, including a huge one for himself, and then, every Friday night, instead of going to synagogue like Jewish men and boys would have done in the old days, we marched around in the gymnasium at P.S. 11 and attempted to become Boy Scouts of America.

My Aunt Rose, who was hardly ever venturing out of her house, used to watch at her window every Friday night to see Lenny appear on the street in his Boy Scout uniform. Except when Marty appeared and whisked her away in his big car, this became the highlight of her week. She used to shout out the window, in her mock-aristocratic, high-pitched, Eleanor Roosevelt voice, "Boy Scouts of Amerricaaa . . ." and then laugh loud and lyrically until tears came into her eyes.

The Scouts were fun for a while, but somehow, I'm afraid that being a scout in The Bronx could never quite capture the old Teddy Roosevelt essence of the endeavor.

For one thing, to be a scout, at a minimum you needed woods. And, as I said before, in The Bronx we didn't even have trees. The big event for our troop was the yearly hike. We all met at the Bronx County Trust Company on Ogden Avenue and then, with my uncle and Reuben in the lead, we set off on our long-awaited adventure which consisted of walking across the George Washington Bridge to Fort Lee, New Jersey, just at the other end. Then we walked through the town for about a half-mile until we came to trees, at which point we left the road, set up our camp, built fires, and cooked bacon and fried potatoes for lunch. Alas, dear reader, if you are a mere city person, you don't know the delight, the sheer primitive ecstasy, of cooking your own lunch, pioneer fashion, in the wilds of Fort Lee, New Jersey, after a strenuous hike across the George Washington Bridge.

"The most important thing about a hike, boys," my uncle would tell us, "is don't wear sneakers. You need support for your feet. We're going into another state now. We're not just going over to Manhattan."

Of course, on the day of the hike, Seymore Melnick showed up in sneakers and we all had a good laugh at his expense, convinced he wasn't going to make it and imagining some weird scout trick coming into play, a trick that only seasoned scouts knew about, like forming teams of Melnick bearers, arms locked in a secret scout grip, to carry Melnick back to The Bronx so we could boast we had made it back without losing a man.

Melnick was used to being laughed at. He had a lustrous fame in the neighborhood for one recurring act. He lived on the fourth floor. Whenever his mother forbade him to do something, he climbed over the railing of his fire escape and hung from it until she reneged. He was an imbecile, but as we got older we still liked to hang out at his house, because his mother had large breasts that always threatened to pop out from the low-cut blouses she wore. My Cousin Louie had a crush on her for years.

My Uncle Lenny continued to take my cousins and me on various trips, now adding a few members of our patrol and taking them along too under the aegis of the Scouts. Our favorite excursions occurred in the winter when he took us to swim in the pool at the Hotel St. George in Brooklyn. There was a gymnasium there. At some point he would always leap on Herbie and put various locks and grips on him, my uncle roaring with delight and naming each hold with a fantastic name of his own invention, tumbling Herbie around the mat and keeping him helpless while Herbie would grumble, "Ah, Pop, come on." He didn't really mind.

To get to Brooklyn we had to take the Seventh Avenue I.R.T. at 181st in Manhattan. "The deepest subway in the world," my uncle used to call it. You had to take an elevator about three flights down to get to track level. My uncle always used to lecture us on the Scout motto, *Be prepared.* "If you learn nothing else from scouting, boys, remember, *be prepared.* That's the sum and substance of it. Be prepared."

One day on a trip to Brooklyn my uncle became so involved in giving us advice about life while we waited at the subway change booth for the elevator to come up to us, that when the elevator doors opened he spun around and jauntily stepped in, not noticing that for some reason the elevator car itself had remained below.

He, who had made the *New York Daily News* when he helped Tiny Nizell capture the gunman, made it that evening for the second of his three times:

EX-HERO FALLS 50 FT.
INTO IRT—LIVES

This became one of the great legends of our neighborhood once we knew my uncle was going to survive, having merely broken his legs. My Cousin Herbie would tell it again and again in later years as our friends stood on the corner in front of the Noonan Plaza and passed the time by swapping comic stories.

"Hey, remember the time my old man fell down the subway?" And we would all gather round expectantly as he began to repeat this great local mythic tale. These tales formed a body of lore about our neighborhood. Everyone told them again and again. They defined us as a people by providing us with a common set of references and they were condensed, exaggerated, and clarified over the years as they were told and retold. They also gave us a sense of dignity. We couldn't sit around a fire describing great hunts or acts of bravery in the wild. We couldn't even pass along great verbal constructs—poetic gems such as immortal descriptions of unforgettable sunsets. We couldn't afford sunsets. With all the tall apartment houses reaching up on all sides, we were lucky to have any sky at all.

All we had were stories of people. People like Herbie's mother Fanny who had once laid out Muriel Teitner with a left hook to the jaw on the sidewalk in front of our building after Muriel had called her a "fishmarket woman." People who we thought were more colorful than the people in places where they did have woods and sunsets. And if we couldn't have the bravest and most noble persons for our tales, we could have the craziest and funniest. We could come to feel that The Bronx might not be everything one could desire, but we took pride in our belief that, "A Nebraska guy wouldn't last here a week."

And if our stories weren't the grandest, we believed they were the funniest, and so our mythology became comic, centered on people, a series of colorful comic characters behaving in improbable ways which might seem incredible to outsiders but which were daily life for us. And the people we valued most were the comic storytellers, those brave people who could, by the mere use of language, assuage the grit and chafe of our lives with healing laughter.

One of our greatest comic storytellers was my Aunt Rose. She was even more noted for her mimicry. She did screamingly funny imitations of everyone: Eleanor Roosevelt, rabbis, all the neighborhood characters. She had the knack of seeing and then replicating the artifice and odd characteristics in people's behavior and speech.

Her favorite imitation at that time was one she did of old Mrs. Weiss, my former babysitter who stuttered and thought I was a genius. Whenever anyone said I was smart, my aunt would hobble after me like old Mrs. Weiss, kissing the top of my head and saying, "Oy, is d-d-dat a D-D-Danny! Is d-d-dat a D-D-Danny!"

What I liked best about my aunt's impersonations was the generous spirit in which they were carried out. She saw people's eccentricities and foibles, she saw them *so* clearly, and yet she saw their humanity as well. There was always a hint of love implicit in such close observation, in the taking on of another persona, however briefly. But how lonely, to see so much.

At home, Aunt Rose was a true comedienne, but totally passive and submissive in the face of the world. Perhaps here lies one clue as to why she gradually began to withdraw from the world. Of course she had been trained since birth to wait for her Prince Charming to rescue her from her tower, and this subtly told her that her fate was not in her own hands and gave the suitors who did show up unwarranted power over her, but on another level I think she saw through social games too easily, and what began for her as a view of life as being a comic masque turned eventually, after the advent of the Nazis and various personal disappointments, into a vision of the world outside her immediate sphere as a kind of cruel theater of the absurd.

She never felt she had a place in the society in which she lived, and she never met other women like herself to give her strength and to relieve her terrible sense of failure and isolation. She had been born with the gift or wound of seeing through facades, and she had never met anyone who could help her build something to put in their place.

Chapter 17

In the spring of my sixth grade year, after a basketball game at P.S. 11 between sixth and seventh grade boys, we decided to form an all-star team to play against boys from others schools.

All the boys on the team had nicknames: Midge Waxenthal (later to become the Giant's batboy), Fat Heshie Jankowitz, Lobo Fox, Needle-nose Noodleman, Sonny Eisenstein, Skinny Diamond, and Huge Marvin Gelman, who had already begun to sprout up to what would soon be six foot five.

Immediately after we formed the team, we called a meeting and saw the possibility of widening our association into a full-fledged club. At this point, another adult came into our lives. His name was Clarence "Pop" Goldman. He wasn't anybody's father. He lived by himself over in the East Bronx. He was a familiar figure in the neighborhood. Everyone had called him Pop for as long as anyone could remember. In his late fifties, he was a small, quiet man with a merry twinkle in his blue eyes. Always friendly and well-mannered to all, Pop was respected by everyone. He was an optometrist, he always wore an old-fashioned suit and tie, and, without asking anything in return, he had organized and led boy's clubs in the neighborhood for years.

It was Midge Waxenthal who brought him to us. Midge's older brother, Peanuts Waxenthal, had been a member of one of Pop's clubs. When Pop had been visiting their family one evening Midge had told him about our incipient organization and Pop had volunteered to lead it.

We had another meeting and Pop presented his plan to us. We would be not merely a team, but an S.A.C. This was the height of prestige at the time. S.A.C. meant Social and Athletic Club and we all wanted to belong to such an organization. Lobo Fox spoke for all of us when he said, enthusiastically, "Anyone can form a team. But with an S.A.C. when we get older we can hire a hall and have parties and dances and hire bands and stuff."

We loved the idea. Of course we never did hire a band or rent a hall, but we did field good teams in three sports and we considered ourselves an S.A.C. and we were proud of the title.

As for the name of the club, Pop suggested we continue the neighborhood tradition of people like Peanuts Waxenthal and his friends by taking the name of their S.A.C., now disbanded since the boys had grown up and gone to work. The name of their team was the Philadelphians.

At first we wondered about the logic of calling ourselves the Philadelphians. Wouldn't people assume we were from Philadelphia? But Pop explained that the reason for the name was that Philadelphia was the city of brotherly love, and that with a name like this we would be unbeatable because we would play together like brothers. This reasoning was irresistible, and when he added, "Not only that, but if you take my old club's name, I'll speak to Peanuts and the guys and I think I can talk them into letting you use their colors, too. Maroon and gold. You boys will be part of a great tradition."

It sounded almost too good to be true. Part of a tradition, a band of brothers, going to various neighborhoods in The Bronx, winning games in the name of brotherly love, and with a respected and established leader to boot. We voted immediately and unanimously constituted ourselves: The Philadelphians S.A.C. of The Bronx, New York.

When I went home and told my parents, my father didn't seem all that happy. He had that look on his face which I would see so clearly when I asked him for a record player a month later.

"A record player? No! And don't ask me again. No, no, no, no, no! Not in a million years!"

"Why not, Dad?"

"Because the next thing you'll want is records."

Yes, he had that look on his face, but my mother read it and said,

"Will there be dues, Danny?"

"Twenty-five cents a week. We're going to get uniforms."

"You see," my father said to her.

"Twenty-five cents, Sid . . . It's nothing. They need clubs. It'll keep them out of trouble. And they'll be associated with Pop Goldman. He's a terrific example for the boys. Everyone speaks highly of him."

"Yeah, yeah," my father said, not impressed.

"And we're not just going to be an independent club," I said. "Pop is going to get us affiliated with the Princes of Syracuse."

"What's the Princes of Syracuse?" my father said.

"Gee . . . I don't know, Dad . . . I thought you would know . . ."

"Never heard of them," he said, and went back to reading Leonard Lyons in the evening paper.

During the days that followed, we organized the club, but I found out that neither of my cousins knew what the Princes of Syracuse was either. After the next meeting, we went up to Pop and asked.

"The Princes of Syracuse? You boys don't know what the Princes of Syracuse are?"

"No, Pop."

"Well boys, you're in for a surprise. The Princes of Syracuse are the youth auxilliary of the Knights of Pythias," he said with pride.

We all nodded and smiled. When he left, I asked my cousins, "What's the Knights of Pythias?"

"I don't know," Louie said. "I thought you would know, Herbie."

"Me? How should I know? I thought you guys knew."

The three of us shared a good laughter together.

Chapter **18**

While I was doing well in school and anticipating beginning junior high, my Aunt Rose was going downhill, alternating between days of being swept away by her prince in his large automobile and weeks of solitary lethargy. Then one day there was a family crisis. Bernie and Bessie and my parents all went over to my Aunt Rose's apartment. When they emerged two hours later my mother had tears in her eyes and my father was looking grim.

Then my Aunt Rose, disheveled and weeping, appeared at our door. She burst into the apartment, saying, "I want it. I want to have it."

"You can't, Rose," my mother said. "Even Bernie and Bessie agree. How can you support it?"

"Marty will support it. He'll come back."

"That rotten son of a bitch was transferred to Elkhart, Indiana," my father said.

"He'll come back. I know he will."

"Why do you think that rotten son of a bitch got transferred in the first place?"

"I'll support it myself. With my money from the buildings."

"Rose," my father said, sadly, "please, be reasonable. The buildings are already mortgaged to support you. They don't provide that much any more. We're going to have to take smaller shares as we go on just to support you."

"I don't care," my aunt said, desperately, putting her face into her hands, sitting on the piano bench, crying. "I don't care. I want it. This is my last chance. I want it . . ."

"It'll just take a couple days," my mother said. "Bernie already talked to the doctor. As far as anyone knows, you just had an appendectomy."

"I want it."

"Think of the family," my mother said, sharply, distraught and weeping herself now.

"*The family*? I want it. It's mine . . ."

"Rose, please," my father said, gently. "There's no money."

"And it's no picnic," my mother said. "You'd be the talk of the block. They wouldn't give you a minute's peace. And you've never worked a day in your life. Believe me, once you have kids, and you see how much work it is, you wonder if it's worth it. And then when they get old, they'll leave you anyway. Believe me, Rose."

"I don't care. I want it. It's mine."

She looked at my father with such a lost, sad, woebegone look in her eyes that he stood up and walked out of the room. My mother sat down next to Rose on the piano bench, put her arm around her shoulders and said, softly, "Don't worry, Rose. You've got plenty of time. You're still a young girl."

Rose sat there, a frightened look on her face now, staring off into space, her left hand in a fist up at her mouth as she gnawed on the exposed side of her index finger with her remaining teeth.

Chapter **19**

After my aunt's "appendectomy," she was continuously depressed. I would see her at her window all day, watching the life on the street and nibbling on candy bars. Finally July came, and we headed to the country for the summer. Uncle Lenny and his family and Uncle Bernie and his family went with us. We left the hot city where the sole activities available for kids in the summer were to go catch polio with the gentiles at Cascades' Pool, or to play knock-hockey all afternoon at the recreation center at P.S. 104. We headed for the country, for trees and open spaces and fresh air. Rose stayed behind.

We went to Ha-Ya Bungalows, about twenty-three miles north of New York City near the town of Nyack. Ha-Ya Bungalows consisted of forty hand-made shacks on two and a half acres of land. The bungalows were owned by Vincent Baglione who had built them with his four sons. The Bagliones were the only gentiles there. All the tenants were Jewish.

My mother had always asked Aunt Rose to visit us but she had rarely come in the past. There was no place for her to stay overnight and she felt out of place since there were no unmarried adults there. After her appendectomy, she never came at all.

One person who did visit us was Pop Goldman. Pop would show up at Ha-Ya wearing his old-fashioned suit even in the summer, coming on the bus because he had no car. We kids looked up to Pop, but at the same time he seemed a trifle odd, not being interested in sports even though he led boys' clubs, and sometimes we would joke about him. He was balding and claimed to have been an eagle scout, so we used to refer to him when he wasn't around as a bald eagle scout.

Pop was known to everyone at the bungalow colony. He said little, just sat there and twinkled. He was part of the family when he was there, and since it seemed to make him so happy to be with us, it made us happy to be part of our family too.

One day, my father, along with several other men, drove our kids' softball team to play a game at Hyenga Lake Bungalows. When we had played them earlier in the summer, they had beaten us 7-4. They had a shortstop named, coincidentally, Donny Schwartz, who was no relative of ours. He had been pretty much a one-man team in that game, going four for five and batting in five runs. The kids on the teams were supposed to be fourteen and under, but Donny was a ringer. He was easily sixteen and he was some kind of big deal in their colony. They had a cheerleading squad of teenage girls who would shout:

> Donny, Donny, he's our man,
> If he can't do it,
> No one can.

Donny loved it. He was exactly the kind of guy that certain teenage girls adore and boys hate.

For our second game with them, we also travelled to their field since we had none of our own. When we started, I was surprised to see my father behind the pitcher, umpiring.

I was playing shortstop. My Cousin Louie pitched. We played fast-pitch—balls and strikes. My Cousin Herbie was in left field. Herbie was a maddening player. He would generally catch the ball, but he would give you a heart attack in the process. In the first inning Donny Schwartz came up and hit a towering fly that was very deep but playable. Herbie took two steps in, then he looked up in panic and started running out, then he turned, took a step in, lunged back and caught it one-handed. When we kidded him about it on the bench, he said, "Whaddya mean? I caught it, didn't I?" And I guess he was right. He was actually good, if you didn't mind suffering a heart attack once in a while as he vacillated in the field. He was a solid hitter. In the third inning he singled to right, I doubled down the left field line scoring him, and my Cousin Louie singled to center scoring me.

When Donny Schwartz returned to the plate it was still 2-0. There were two men on base and two out. The girls went crazy. But Donny was over-anxious, swinging at the first pitch which was in the dirt. He had tried to check his swing but had gone all the way around. My father called it a strike. Donny, embarrassed, began to taunt my father. Louie was pitching him carefully. The next pitch was up at his eyes.

"Ball one," my father said.

"Ball?" Donny said, sarcastically. "Why don't you call that one a strike, too? Why don't you get a new pair of glasses?"

"Just swing the bat, wise guy."

"You're the one who's a bat. You're blind as a bat," Donny said, wittily, as the girls, and in fact, the whole crowd of spectators, laughed.

"Play ball!" my father said.

On the next pitch, Donny hit a smash on the ground right past the pitcher. My father hopped out of the way just in time. I moved to my left behind the bag at second and somehow it stuck in the webbing of my glove. I flipped it backhanded to Mike Blumberg covering second for the force-out to end the inning.

Donny was furious. At me, my father, at everyone on our team. It was mostly an accident that Mike had been at second and we all knew it. He had merely run over to his right after the ball, had pretty much wound up on second by chance. He had caught my throw as a form of self-defense when it came at him. Mike was not the best ballplayer around, and, in fact, you could say he was a bit of a moron. When he spoke, all he ever said was one sentence over and over again in a black accent: "Lukie, you done put the ball in your pocket." No matter what you said to him, he answered in a slow drawl, "Lukie, you done put the ball in your pocket."

So when Donny said to him, as Mike came off the field, "You were lucky, jerk," Mike said to him, "Lukie, you done put the ball in your pocket." My father laughed and this made Donny even more furious. He yelled at my father, "I almost got you that time," and he laughed.

My father merely said, "Sure, sure, play ball!" But the fact that Donny was claiming to have tried to hit him with the ball wasn't lost on him. Somewhere inside himself, perhaps on a completely subconscious level, he would be watching now to see that Donny didn't drift over into that forbidden territory called "taking advantage of my good nature."

In the sixth inning we got another run to lead 3-0. Donny was getting progressively more angry. In the last of the sixth he came up to bat with the bases loaded and two out. Since it was only a seven-inning game, this was Hyenga's big chance. The crowd was wild. "Come on, Donny! Home run!" the girls shouted.

He stepped up to the plate looking like a right-handed Ted Williams. A killer. He continued to berate my father as my father called two balls ("Why not a strike, you bat?") and a strike. ("Strike? Are you blind? We know what side you're on.") And then he got under a high inside pitch and fouled it off down the third base line toward the woods that rimmed the field. I chased it from my shortstop posi-tion, running away from the plate and getting under it as I ran into the woods at full speed and caught it as I tripped over a tree, rolled over, but came up with the ball still in my glove.

Donny continued to stand at the plate, ready for his next swing, ready to hit the big home run. He couldn't seem to grasp what had happened. The weak hitters would follow in the last of the seventh. But I had caught the ball, and the game was effectively over.

"He never caught that ball!" he shouted at my father. "He never caught it! He dropped it!" A few people joined him, but most knew I had held the ball and the protest died away except for Donny who was out of his mind, yelling at my father, "You're favoring your son. You're favoring your son, you jerk."

My father was angry, but he knew it was an umpire's lot to be yelled at so he kept his temper. When I came up to the plate, the first pitch was outside.

"Ball one."

"Ball?" Donny shouted. "That caught the outside corner."

The next pitch was up at my eyes.

"Ball two."

"Ball two? You bum! You're favoring your son, you bum!"

Here was where Donny made his mistake. First of all he had the audacity, the sheer effrontery, to suggest that my father would actually favor his own son over anyone else in the world, and second, he called my father by that single epithet which was his nightmare-name, his shadow, his haunted spectre of grievous failure—*a bum*.

My father moved off the mound toward the third base line, walking quickly at a determined pace. Everyone wondered what he was up to. He seemed furious but controlled, walking with steady purpose but *away* from Donny Schwartz who was at shortstop. At the baseline he calmly picked up a bat, turned, raised it over his head like a tomahawk, and began to walk *toward* Donny. And somehow the fact that he was walking, walking quickly, but nevertheless still walking, made his actions even more frightening than if he had simply charged Donny.

Donny looked at my father with an expression that said, "Are you kidding?" but when he saw my father's face he blanched and turned and began to trot out toward left center field, saying over his shoulder, "Hey, come on . . . Come on . . . ," trying not to seem to be running in fear but running nonetheless as my father walked quickly after him, saying, with gritted teeth, "I'm gonna kill you, boy. Boy, I'm gonna kill you."

Now Donny just took off, running toward center field. The Hyenga crowd went crazy, the girls and women screaming, the other players on the team scattering, as the Hyenga men grabbed bats and burst out from the stands, running to a position between my father and Donny who was now over toward right center field.

At this point two of our men who had also run onto the field grabbed my father from behind and held him there with his bat still up in the air like a hatchet. My father didn't resist. He felt he had already won. He had this wild smile on his face as he stared at Donny, terrified in right field. He hardly noticed the Hyenga men coming at *him* with bats. At this moment my Uncle Lenny arrived. He got between my father and the approaching hoarde and he began, incredibly, to shadowbox, facing the Hyenga men, dancing around there on the grass in front of my father, going "Haw! Haw! Haw!" as he threw combinations into the air, like a punch-drunk fighter, seemingly oblivious to everybody, but throwing punches like a crazed machine, "Haw! Haw! Haw!" bobbing and weaving, a lone figure out there in the outfield.

Well, now the Hyengas began to have second thoughts. Suddenly they recognized they were dealing with a heavy-duty situation here, and that, although they clearly outnumbered our men, they knew that if they attacked, the two men who were holding my father would release him and they would be confronted by an obvious berserko with a bat and a *meshuggener* boxer who was still dancing around throwing lefts and rights into the air and going, "Haw! Haw! Haw!"

The men stopped and stood there facing each other. Then one of the men on their side said, "What kind of thing is that? A Jewish man running after a kid with a bat?"

"That's some 'kid,'" my father said.

"Yeah, he's probably got two kids of his own already," Herbie said from behind my father.

"You shut up," my Uncle Lenny said.

"You just get outa here, Buster," one of the Hyenga men said, raising up his bat and gesturing toward my father, "and don't come back." But the man didn't advance.

"Let's go," my uncle said.

We backed off toward the parking lot, facing the men from Hyenga as we proceeded, slowly, with my father with his bat and my uncle as our first line of defense, keeping the Hyenga men off us as they followed us to our cars, bats raised, but keeping a safe distance away.

Chapter **20**

In the fall, I entered Junior High School 82. The greatest
source of danger in this school was a moron named Terry Rafferty
who attempted to rob us each morning. He lay in wait for us on
Featherbed Lane. Rafferty was frightening looking. He had been left
back twice and he had little pointed ears that seemed pinned back
to his head, along with small beady eyes which made him look like
a large malevolent rodent, mean and merciless. And he was.

Each morning he would try to steal my single most important
possession—my lunch money. Lunch was no joking matter to me at
that time. It was the highlight of my day between breakfast and dinner.
A typical lunch for me began with the hot plate at the school
cafeteria—say meat loaf, mashed potatoes, peas, two pieces of bread
and butter, a side order of potatoes, a container of milk and a piece
of cake. Then I would go outside to the nearby stores to get still another
order of potatoes, my third, this time french fried, with a large coke,
and then an ice cream.

So my lunch money was a serious matter. Before we encountered
Rafferty each morning, I took off my shoes and hid my money in them.
Then he would appear, like a troll.

"Hey, loan me thirty cents?"

"I don't have it, Rafferty."

"All the money I find on you I keep?"

If you said no here, he would beat the shit out of you for lying
to him, so you had to let him search you. But he never thought to

search your shoes. It probably never occurred to him that he had enough power to make a person go through the complicated procedure of taking off his shoes twice each morning. After he released me, I would hobble away, hoping the coins wouldn't jingle as they cut into the bottoms of my feet.

As Rafferty got older, he continued his weird and frightening ways. There was something about his pin-headed dementia that no one liked to mess with. One thing we learned in The Bronx was the sheer power of naked, unadulterated, irrational force. You learned early that if you were going to get through life, you were going to have to pay certain tolls. There was a point beyond which you had to let go of ideas of justice and notions of dignity and individual rights and give up a lunch or a jacket if you wanted to keep your teeth.

My Cousin Louie never seemed to learn this lesson. He would have grabbed Rafferty and beat the shit out of him, probably getting stabbed in the process. But as a mook, he was a special case.

Louie's outrageous bravado sometimes made it dangerous to be with him. Most of the time it was safe because local guys knew his "rep" and wouldn't tangle with him. They knew he would take a few of them with him to the hospital if he was attacked. But sometimes being with Louie in collision with people who didn't know him was totally hair-raising.

Once, the two of us were walking home from a Yankee game, through Jerome Park, when we passed three guys one of whom turned back and shouted at us, "Fuck your mother."

Well, I thought, we got out of that one fairly easily. One "Fuck your mother" won't harm anyone, sticks and stones, etc. But just as I was breathing easier, Louie turned around and shouted after them, "What was that?"

"You heard me, jerk."

"What did you say?"

"Fuck your mother."

"Fuck *my* mother?"

Well, here the three guys were getting worried. They didn't know us, but they could see we were not the smallest people in the world, and here was this one guy clearly challenging them even though they had us outnumbered three to two, and there was no one else around. On the surface, it seemed as if they could stomp the shit out of us with no one there to interfere, a fact of which I was well aware. But this didn't bother Louie at all, and somehow this confused the three guys. Even frightened them. I mean, who *was* this crazy guy and what did he have behind him? Was he carrying a rod? Was he just out of the joint or something? Who *was* he?

At that moment, just as they were beginning to feel the slightest sliver of doubt, Louie charged like an enraged bull, shouting, "Fuck *whose* mother?" He stormed right at the three guys who, astonishingly, were so dumbfounded they ran away. And Louie chased them across the park, not merely trying to flush them and drive them off, but actually trying to *catch* them. Finally he stopped and shouted after them, "Fuck my mother, hah? I'll give you a fuck my mother, you jerks."

Incidents like that used to occur all the time with Louie. That's why he was a mook. That's what mooks do and why they're so hard to understand.

Back in junior high, my Cousin Herbie had his own way of saving face and strengthening his ego after Rafferty and other morons inflicted daily humiliations upon us. He would wait until after school was over and then, on the way home, he would beat up on kids who were younger than he was. This was exhilarating and I used to do it, too.

We would walk past P.S. 104 which only went up to the sixth grade. As we strolled along the sidewalk near our old school, crowded with smaller kids going in the other direction, we would bump into them and knock their books down. It seemed good, clean, harmless, fun.

Then one day when my cousin wasn't with me I decided to knock a few books down on my own. I sideswiped a couple sixth graders, toppling their texts, and then BAM! I got hit from behind with a tremendous shot in the ear. Even before I could turn, painfully, to see who had slammed me, my situation became instantly clear to me—some part of me must have known all along that I had overlooked Hammerhead Morgan who still went to P.S. 104. Yes, Willie Hammerhead Morgan! He who threw the fire ax at my Cousin Herbie in the Zenith Theater. He of thirty other famous incidents of violence against all and sundry. I quickly realized that I was not, in fact, older than every kid in P.S. 104. Hammerhead was two years older than I, he was a maniac, he was still in elementary school, and I had invaded his turf and had violated his serfs whom he had to protect. I was in for it.

"You like to knock kids' books down, eh?"

"Who me, Willie?"

"No, a Chinaman. Who else, jerk?"

"Oh, I thought you meant my Cousin Herbie."

"Fuck your cousin. I'll get him when I see him. Right now I'm dealing with you, jerk-off." He flicked his finger against my ear, the one he had just punched, as if he were flicking off a fly. It stung. I reached up and covered it with my hand. A crowd of sadistic little kids gathered around. They wanted to see me get my comeuppance. And worst of all, I realized they were right. What had seemed like fun, following my cousin, now appeared in another light. I was in the worst situation I could imagine. I was up against Hammerhead and he was right. And I knew even back then how people like Hammerhead act when they are finally and undeniably in a situation in which they are right.

"So, you like to pick on people who are littler than you."

"Who me? Why should I pick on little kids?"

BAM! Hammerhead moved in, throwing punches to my midsection, backing me up against the wall, shouting insanely, "Little kids! You pick on little kids! Little kids who never hurt no one!" and with each foot and meter of his rhythmic prose, he would slam me in the stomach, left right left, "*Little kids!* (right) *Innocent little kids!* (left)"

I was in a terrible dilemma. I was trying to defend myself, but Hammerhead was bigger, stronger, and he had the psychological advantage of being a known and confirmed lunatic. So I was trying to block his punches but the thing I feared most was that somehow I might hurt *him*. Because if I did, if I threw a lucky punch that landed, Hammerhead would end my short life on Earth. No more Cadeco-Ellis All-Star Baseball games, no more three orders of potatoes for lunch, no more dreams of playing for the Yankees, *caput, shoyn* and *fartig, gounisht,* I'd be through.

So I was actually relieved when I went down and Hammerhead got on top of me. There was now a huge crowd watching as everyone had yelled, "Fight! Fight! Fight!" to attract a mob, and he had each kid come up one at a time and spit in my face.

I got out of there lucky. You can wipe spit off your face. You can shake off the effects of 67 body punches in a few days. You don't have to go to Morrisania Hospital and explain to the doctor why you have a six-foot-long fire ax sticking out of your shoulder.

When I saw my Cousin Herbie later that day, I warned him to stay away from P.S. 104, and to cool it on picking on the little kids.

"*Hammerhead's* after me?" he said.

"You know it."

"Gee, that's funny. How'd he know it was me? I mean he never saw me."

"Beats me," I said. "Someone must've told him."

Chapter 21

I did moderately well in the seventh grade, but I can't say I really liked my new school. It wasn't exactly the kind of place where the principal would come around to our class and play the accordion or where Tonto would show up to sing and dance for us in our assembly.

One day, when I arrived at school, there were several big tough guys there from De Witt Clinton, an all-boys high school. It turned out they were "on strike" for some reason, and they had fanned out to the junior high schools to seek support from the boys. The way we were to show we supported their strike was to break the rules of our school by taking off our ties. They formed inspection committees at the gates to the schoolyard. If you had taken off your tie, they let you pass. If you hadn't, they pulled out a large scissors and cut your tie off.

I loved this. It seemed so impressive to me. A boy supports your strike, fine. A boy doesn't support your strike, you cut his tie in half. It was so direct. So romantic. No formal authorities, no technicalities, no principals and assistant principals to ask whether it was legal or not. And these guys were rough. Even Terry Rafferty didn't mess with them.

From that day on, I knew I would go to De Witt Clinton High School.

During this period, my Aunt Rose continued to stay in her house. I would visit her at times, but all she seemed to say was, "Why was I born?" Her boyfriend, Marty, had never returned. She had stopped cooking for herself, and she subsisted merely on sandwiches from Manny's luncheonette or from the delicatessen. Sandwiches and sweets. And rather than go out to get them, she would give some kid a big tip for bringing them to her apartment.

No longer would she joke with Jack Rabinowitz, the thirty-five-year-old "newsboy" when he would flirt with her. No longer would she tell him to go home and "play with your yo-yo."

No longer would she come over to our apartment and sing, "There'll be blue birds over the white cliffs of Dover," while my mother accompanied her on the piano.

I slowly expanded my territory, no longer wary of going into the territory of Ronoso on the next block, or frightened of the Shakespeare Tong.

On the other hand, we still had our territorial limits. If our new range was slightly larger, the people on its fringes were older and more dangerous. And even in our own neighborhood, there were still pockets of forbidden territory. The evening center at P.S. 11 was taken over by the Ikes, who wouldn't let outsiders go there to play pool or ping-pong. At one point, when he was in high school, my Cousin Herbie actually went over there one night, determined to assert his right to shoot pool in a public center.

The Ikes did let him shoot pool. He was feeling exhilarated. A hero who had gone out and conquered the dragons. But when he left they were waiting for him on an empty, dark street. They pulled a little trick that amused them. They had an extremely short moron walk up and bump into him. Then they all gathered around and accused him of picking on a little guy. Then they grabbed him and held him while the little guy worked him over. When he fell to the ground they stomped on him until, bleeding from the mouth and face, he staggered home in the dark.

Harlem was south-west of our neighborhood. We were separated from it by the river and we didn't have too much trouble with the gangs there except for incidents in the area of the bridge between the Polo Grounds and Yankee Stadium. One day my Cousin Louie and I came out of a Yankee game and walked over to McCombs Dam Park. There were about fifteen black kids on one sandlot field when two teams from our neighborhood, the Saints and the Bronx Cardinals, showed up to play a game of hardball. They summarily kicked the black kids off the field. When the black kids, who were about twelve years old, complained, they picked up bats and chased the black kids over toward the bridge to Harlem.

Louie and I sat down behind home plate. The Saints had a pitcher, Joey LaBocca, who was locally famous, so we thought we'd watch for a while. The field was enclosed by a high fence with only one doorway, in right field. We were outside the fence, which was fortunate, because about an hour later a large moving van pulled up to the curb just outside the doorway in the fence. Two of the black kids who had been playing on the field hopped out of the cab of the truck, pointed to the guys from our neighborhood, and shouted, "That's them."

At this point, the driver honked his horn twice, the back of the van flew open, and about thirty guys came flying out with bats and lead pipes. They ran through the entrance to the field and began to do a number on both teams. Some of the Bronx boys actually made it over the twenty-foot fence in their panic but most were trapped inside. It was terrible to watch but we didn't stick around. Having no friends on either side, we just got out of there as quickly as we could, which goes to prove that even a mook like Louie could act rationally once in a while, if he was not emotionally involved in what was going on.

The guys from Harlem pulled this stunt once more when we were older. It involved a guy named "the Mad German" who went to Taft High School in our neighborhood. He had a weapon he had designed that looked like a huge fountain pen but that shot bullets. I had heard of him from Fat Heshie Jankowitz who went to Taft. Once, in the boys' bathroom, the Mad German had come up to Heshie and said, "You see this pen? I bet you don't believe it's a gun."

"Who me?"

"No, Chiang Kai-shek."

"What?"

"This pen. I bet you don't believe it's a gun."

"Why should I doubt your word?"

"You really believe it's a gun?"

"Sure. Why not if you say so?"

"Well, you're right!" the Mad German said, and he pressed a

button and fired a bullet into the wall just over Heshie's head.

A few months later he tried a similar trick on a black kid on the street. When the black guy said, "Don't you ever try none of your shit on me again," he reloaded and shot the kid in the arm. The kid wasn't hurt badly but he couldn't get revenge because the Mad German had a gang of followers. Then one afternoon, as the Mad German and about eight of his friends left school, a large van rolled up and half of Harlem ran out and did a job on them with pipes and bats.

My mother's maid, Roxie, lived in Harlem. She would come up on the subway one day a week to iron and clean the house. I liked her. She listened to blues and gospel music on the radio and she was always kind to me. She was two or three years older than my mother and my mother always said, "I love her like a sister. The other women are fit to be tied that I got her because I treat her so nice. They don't like it that I pay her subway fare when she comes here. They say I spoil her. But I don't care what they say. Maybe I'm too good. I don't know. But *shvartzes* are human, too. Believe me there are plenty of *goyem* that are a lot worse."

One day I came home from school to find my mother and Roxie in the kitchen. Roxie was ironing and my mother was at the table sipping on a cup of coffee and looking at some photos.

"Hey, Danny, come over here for a second. Look at these pictures."

The photos were of abstract sculpture, about three feet high, made of dozens of knives, knives painted in various colors.

"Roxie's son made these statues. Aren't they beautiful? Tell the truth."

"Yeah, Ma. I like them. They really say something."

Roxie smiled. She was pleased that we liked the photos but you could tell she wasn't all that certain about them herself.

"Her son is a genius," my mother said. "A genius! If he got a break, he'd be famous."

Later that evening, when we were by ourselves, I said to my mother, "Do you really think Roxie's son is a good artist, Ma?"

"*Artist*? That *meshuggener* is a dope addict. He makes these knife statues in his therapy. Can you believe it? He's already a dope addict. So what do they give him to get better? Knives! And the state pays for it."

"I don't know . . . They weren't bad . . ."

"I'll say one thing, better he should put the knives in statues than in people. But he's breaking his mother's heart. A mother's heart is easily broken and don't you forget that. That's what rotten kids do. They break their mother's hearts. That's why I thank God every night I got a kid like you. Brilliant, kind," she kissed my head, "he wouldn't harm a flea. Not a flea, he's so nice. And your brother, too. I don't play favorites. He might not eat, but he's shrewd as a tack, that *bonditt*. Listen, I just got some new jelly at Daitch's. Strawberry-grape. It just came out. Esther Babbisch tried it and she swears by it. Let me make you a sandwich with some fresh cream cheese on fresh white bread."

Chapter **22**

About nine months before my thirteenth birthday, my parents sat me down for a talk. They wanted me to begin studying for my *bar mitzvah*.

"I don't want a *bar mitzvah*."

"You have to have a *bar mitzvah*," my father said, his tongue bright red from his having eaten a pound of pistachio nuts he had bought at Krums near Fordham Road. "Whaddya mean you don't want a *bar mitzvah*?"

"I don't want one."

"What are you talking about? Every Jewish boy wants a *bar mitzvah*."

"Well I don't. I don't believe in it. That's why I stopped going to Hebrew School when I was eleven. Ask the Rabbi."

"Let's not get into *that*," my mother said.

"A Rabbi deserves respect," my father said. "He's like an army officer. You might not like him personally, but if he's got the rank, he deserves respect. That's why you salute an officer. You're not saluting him. You're saluting the uniform."

"*What?*"

"Look, Danny, never mind that," my mother said. "That's neither here nor there. You gotta have a *bar mitzvah*. It's as simple as that. Have you thought about what the neighbors would say if you didn't? Muriel Teitner and her friends. They're jealous of me already because my father owned the building. You'll be putting ammunition in their hands. Please don't do this to me, Danny."

At this point, I played my hole card. "I'd do it for you but it's too late, Ma. You can't learn your *hoftorah* in nine months."

"There's where you're wrong," she said, smiling. "We found an answer."

The "answer" showed up the next week. He was named Eli Simonson. A nice man, slim, olive-skinned, about thirty-five, with hunched-over shoulders and a gray suit that was too big for him. He looked a little like my Cousin Arthur across the street. Arthur was a year younger than my brother and he had hunched-over shoulders, too. My mother said it was from my Aunt Hilda pounding on his shoulders with her fists when she beat him which was often. Sometimes my aunt beat him when they were on the street and my mother would rush between them, shouting, "Hilda, stop. Are you out of your mind? It's not human to hit a kid like that." And Hilda would start crying and run off to her apartment.

Arthur was later arrested for following women home from foreign movie theaters, but that's another story. The fact is I felt such pity for this Hebrew teacher that I couldn't refuse the lessons. "It would be like taking the bread out of the mouths of his two daughters," my mother said.

I gave it a try. Eli had the world's worst voice. He sounded like a subway train rounding a curve. But this did not stop him from making records of himself singing my *hoftorah*. My father was forced to buy me a phonograph so I could learn the records by heart. I sang along with Eli, not having the faintest idea of what the words meant, but happy to be helping him to feed his daughters and to be pleasing my mother who continued to feed all my friends and to allow us to play ball in the house, an activity which eventually led to the day when, in high school, Skinny Diamond and I triumphed over two all-city basketball players in tally-bell basketball in my bedroom, Ralph Walter who later started for N.Y.U., and Stan Reiner who had to give up competitive basketball after the police found him one night, out in a snow storm in his pajamas, dribbling a basketball down Mt. Eden Avenue at three in the morning in a kind of daze, which resulted in his being put away for a while in a mental hospital.

The memorable event of this spring, the surprise and talk of the neighborhood, occurred when my Uncle Lenny, big, burly, bald,

Lenny, bought a lovely blond cocker spaniel. He named her *shayner* (pretty) which quickly became "Shane D." in practice. Whenever anyone asked him what kind of dog she was, he would smile and say, "She's a pedigreed."

My uncle bought her a jeweled (rhinestone) collar, combed her every day, and would stand with her in front of the building to show her off to passersby. My Aunt Fanny was proud of her too. She made appearances on the street with Lenny and Shane D., wearing her matching rhinestone glasses.

In fact, the only one who didn't like her that much was Herbie. He was slightly jealous of all the attention she got.

In junior high school I began a lifelong love affair with one of the great institutions of the civilized world: the public library. I loved to read but I had a shameful secret: When I was twelve years old I would often take out books marked: For boys from 6 to 10.

After a while I graduated to teenage books, great sports stories about the light and dark blue of Clarkston Prep, John R. Tunis, and dog stories by Albert Payson Terhune. These were the books I liked best: sports and dog stories. *Home Run Hennesey* and *Lad of Sunnybank*. I couldn't get enough of them.

The books we read in school were something else again. In the eighth grade we were introduced to "real literature": *Ivanhoe*.

Ivanhoe! The single most inappropriate book they could have assigned to us. If they had *calculated* how to turn Bronx kids away from literature for the rest of their lives, they couldn't have picked a better method of doing it than to force us to read *Ivanhoe*.

Ivanhoe fulfilled perfectly every negative stereotype we Bronx kids had about literature:

1. Literature was irrelevant to our lives.

2. Literature was written in a weird language that no one spoke.

3. Literature was by and for British people or for rich Americans who pretended to be British.

Now I realize that on some arcane level which I later came to understand, much of what was going on between boys and girls and gangs on the streets of The Bronx derived from ancient medieval codes of honor and chivalry, only vaguely understood and partially passed down along the dark streets of the unconscious of the English-speaking world. But at that time, the book seemed totally foreign to us, snobby, archaic, and forbidding, and no one ever tried to show us its relevance to our situation. "Relevance" was not a concept in education in the '50s Bronx junior high schools.

We weren't acquainted with any people who said "thee" and "thou" and we didn't know any girls named "Rowena." To us, literature seemed to be for lords and ladies and pompous asses, just as opera was the fat soprano from Akron, Ohio, who always finished third on "The Ted Mack Original Amateur Hour." That we were not turned away from books for our entire lives, that some of us like Herbie and myself actually went on to sniff out their treasures on our own, to pass them around and share them like dark and valuable secrets, is a tribute to the indomitable thirst for knowledge in human beings, and to certain perceptive and generous librarians and teachers who understood our needs as street kids. It's also a tribute to the great, lasting, and compelling power of books themselves.

And when I say turned off for life, I'm not exaggerating. For example, my father had an I.Q. of 140 and he never read a book in his life. Not one. In his case, I think he didn't begin early enough. He knew that to be good at reading you had to read many books, and he felt he had fallen too far behind and could never catch up to those who read regularly. He also did not like to be confronted with evidence of what he did not know and of what he had been deprived of in life.

Besides a medical novel now and then, my mother didn't regularly read books. In fact, none of my aunts or uncles, nor any of the adults on our block read books. There was one old lady, Mrs. Feiger, who was the exception that proved the rule. She was reputed to have read Goethe in the original German, and sometimes when she would pass, people would say if the conversation turned to her, "There goes Mrs. Feiger. She read Goethe," although no one really knew anything else about Goethe other than the fact that he was supposed to be "a great author."

But I loved books, and my intuition told me that surely good books couldn't stop with *Lassie Come Home* and the Chip Hilton sports stories. I decided one day to go to the paperback rack at the candy store and buy a "real book" (as opposed to a boys' book).

But where to start? There was no one I could ask. I had to take a chance on my own. I didn't want to risk another *Ivanhoe*, but I did want a book that was a classic. An important, serious, book. So I determined to look for a book which I felt would fulfill these characteristics. I looked for a book by an author who had three names.

Somehow I had gotten the idea that was how one distinguished a serious author from a sham. A real author had three names.

I found such a book and I took it home and I read it. I had heard of the author. I knew he was famous but I found the book disappointing. It set me back in my reading for a while until I gathered the courage to try again.

The book I had bought was by Earl Stanley Gardner.

It was, in part, because of these difficult beginnings, that when I did find books that spoke to me, they made such an extraordinary impression on me. The first was *The Catcher in the Rye*. When I read it I was shocked to realize something I had never known before and it gave me one of the greatest thrills of my life: Literature was about me. It could be written in American. It could be *for* Americans. It could be written by people who might actually understand me better than my own family.

This opened up a new world to me. A new family actually. Because the American novelists I read, on my own, while I was in high school—Willa Cather, F. Scott Fitzgerald, Ernest Hemingway, Thomas Wolfe, James T. Farrell, Carson McCullers, Richard Wright, and others—became my older brothers and sisters. It was to them that I turned for advice, for solace, for enlightenment, and for the repeated lesson that it was possible to be an intelligent, sensitive, and alienated American and to still love the possibilities of America, and somehow, even, to reach out and help other lost and yearning Americans like myself.

This knowledge kept me going through many arduous times. The idea that I might write a book someday—I, a fat, ill-cultured son of a non-literate neighborhood, the grandchild of immigrants who couldn't read or write English—that idea was so farfetched, so impossibly grandiose, that it never even entered my mind.

Chapter **23**

"**Y**our cousins, Louie and Herbie, they had their *bar mitzvahs* on Nelson Avenue. You're gonna have yours on the Concourse," my father said to me on the evening we drove down to rent the hall.

"What's wrong with Nelson Avenue?"

"Who said anything was wrong with Nelson Avenue?" my mother said.

"Oh, well," I said, resignedly, "if I have to have a *bar mitzvah*, at least there's one consolation. At least I'll get a lot of presents."

Suddenly a heavy, unnatural silence settled over us. My father and mother looked at each other, neither wanting to speak. Then my father swallowed and said, "The presents?"

"Yeah. The presents. If I have to go through with this whole thing, at least I'll have the presents. I'll put them in the bank. Maybe I can use them to go to college someday."

There was another deep silence. Then my mother began, "You see, Danny . . ."

When she paused, my father interrupted, "Look, Danny, you see . . . You don't get the presents. It's as simple as that."

"I *don't*?" I said, astonished, "Then who does?"

"I do," my father said.

"*You* do?"

"How do you think I'm gonna pay for this goddamn affair. It's costing me an arm and a leg."

"But . . . They give the presents to me, don't they? Checks?"

"That's right," my father said. "And then you sign them and give them to me so I can record them so I'll know how much to give them back as presents when they have an affair, and then I'll use them to help me pay the bills."

Later, at the temple on the Grand Concourse, near Burnside Avenue, we found out just how much the bills would be. We would have the services in the synagogue on Saturday morning, then a catered affair in the basement of the building that night.

"Do you want roast beef or chicken?" the manager said.

"What's the difference?" my father said.

"Twenty-five cents more for the roast beef."

"They had roast beef at Louie's and chicken at Herbie's," my mother said. "Let's have the roast beef."

"But Ceil, we're talking about 125 people . . ."

"So what. People, schmeople. How many sons do you have? He gets A's in school. He's a brilliant boy. What're you gonna give him? Chicken?"

"Chicken's OK with me, Ma."

"You keep out of this, smart alec," my mother said.

"Don't interrupt your mother," my father said. He turned to the manager. "We'll have roast beef," he said, in a weak voice.

"Good," the manager said, making a note on his pad. "Roast beef it is. You made a smart decision. You'll never regret it. Years from now, you'll say, 'To think, we almost chose chicken to save a few pennies on our son's *bar mitzvah*.' Believe me, people will talk about this affair of yours for years to come. Now, do you want a baked potato or mashed potatoes? Baked potato is ten cents extra," and he turned toward my mother.

And as the bill mounted, as my father committed himself to paying more and more money, as if by some sympathetic reaction, he began to take on the color of money. Slowly but perceptibly, he began to turn green. Finally the manager said, "Of course you'll want the *pièce* de *résistance*. The extra ceremony."

"The extra ceremony?" my father said. He was sick now. He was dying and he hadn't even signed the check for the deposit.

"Oh, no," I said. "No, no, no, no, no. No extra ceremony."

"Wait a minute," my mother said. "Let's at least hear the man out. What ceremony is this, Mr. Nusserman?"

"I don't want any extra ceremony," I said. "The real ceremony in the synagogue in the morning is enough. Please . . . It's just showing off . . . It's corny and fake . . ."

"Quiet," my father said.

"Thank you," Mr. Nusserman said, smiling at my father and ignoring me. "But perhaps I shouldn't have even brought it up. It's really just something for the rich, I guess. Just for the classiest affairs that people will remember for their entire lives. You see, in the evening, while everyone leaves the hall so the waiters can take away the *hors d'oeuvres* and set up the tables for dinner, there's a lull in the proceedings so to speak. So for those few people who can afford something really special, instead of pushing everyone out to wait around in the smokey hallway downstairs, for those few who are successful enough in their chosen professions, for a hundred dollars we have everyone go upstairs to the synagogue and we have another ceremony, not really a religious one, but one where the cantor sings and you walk down the aisle as a family and he blesses your son."

"No, no," I said. "I won't do it."

"Shut up, you," my father said, with a menacing look.

"It's nothing," my mother said to me. "Whaddya want them to do? Stand in the hallway? What's the big deal? Your father is spending a fortune on this for you. More than Herbie and Louie's *bar mitzvah*. Give him a little satisfaction."

"No, I won't do it."

She turned to my father. "Sid, if my mother were alive, this is what she'd want."

"OK," my father said, grimly, "we'll do it."

My mother smiled. "Someday you'll thank us, Danny, believe me. You'll remember this for the rest of your life."

Nusserman wrote quickly on his pad.

"We better go now," my father said, leading us toward the door. "I'll mail you a check for the deposit. Send me an estimate." I could tell he wanted to rush to a candy store to get a Bromo-Seltzer.

"OK. Believe me, you won't regret this decision." As we left, Nusserman added, "Oh, I forgot to ask one more thing. For the final touch for the ceremony. You'll want a soprano in the balcony singing, 'Boy of Mine' for twenty-five bucks, won't you?"

My father nodded yes without saying a word and walked, stoop-shouldered out the door.

The morning religious services of my *bar mitzvah* were painful for me even though I was the star. I felt as if I were party to a fraud. In the first place, I couldn't read the Hebrew language. The only Hebrew word I was certain of was "kosher" and I had learned this on my own from butcher shop windows all over New York. In the second place, I fancied myself an atheist. I simply could not believe that Jehovah, as pictured in the Bible—smiting people, annihilating armies, destroying cities—was really God. He reminded me too much of my father. And in the third place, I honestly did not believe the Jews were the chosen people, in spite of the fact that we Jewish kids always did well on the Stanford-Binet I.Q. Test.

When I stood up to sing my *hoftorah* in the synagogue, I placed a Hebrew book in front of me but I could not read it, I pretended to pray to God although I did not believe in him, and I sang my *hoftorah* with great authority although I didn't have the vaguest idea of what I was saying.

Everyone loved it. They said I had a "terrific voice," that I was "brilliant." The proud mothers seemed all to become my mother, with tears in their eyes. My parents were robustly congratulated by everyone, and I was now "a man in Israel."

I felt wretched. Cheap, fake, and ashamed.

The only part I liked occurred just before noon. There was to be a test of the air raid sirens. The Rabbi announced, at five to twelve, that no one should be disturbed when the sirens (he pronounced it "sireens") blew. This gave my thirteen-year-old friends a lecherous laugh and made me feel somewhat better for a while.

The test of the sirens which interrupted the Rabbi's sermon was part of America's civil defense mania in the '50s. In junior high we all dove under our desks each month on signal to avoid being decimated when the Commies dropped the Big One on New York. "Now boys and girls, remember, don't look at the flash or you'll go blind, and when you do see the flash, dive under your desks so you don't get hit by flying glass or get knocked on the head when the ceiling falls . . ."

They held up huge maps of New York City with concentric circles indicating areas which would sustain different percentages of destruction. Whenever we went through one of these drills, I worried about my father at his liquor store in Manhattan, smack within the 75% destroyed area. I had no doubt I would make it in The Bronx. I would be cut and bruised, but I would make it. But he was down there in Manhattan where the real damage would be done.

My father was not going to make it.

I worried about him much of the time. I felt he was very brave to be sacrificing himself for his family by entering the area of 75% destruction each day. I hoped he had not seen the maps and the percentages. I hoped for his own peace of mind in the meantime that he did not learn that he was doomed.

When I entered high school, I began to worry about myself being doomed. The Korean War was on, full swing. Suppose it lasted until I was eighteen? Would it be my fate to be sent to freezing mountains on the other side of the world to shoot it out with nameless North Koreans before I even had a chance to go off on my own and find out who I was and what I was supposed to do here? Why me? I wondered. I didn't even know how to tell the difference between a North Korean and a South Korean.

But on the day of my *bar mitzvah*, atomic bombs and Koreans were the least of our troubles. My father was in a kind of calm frenzy, trying to appear relaxed and to be having a good time while the engine of his nervous system was idling as if his accelerator had stuck to the floorboard.

In the afternoon, between the services and the affair, my father attempted to teach my Cousin Burt Farber to run his movie camera. My father had taken up home-movie making as a hobby. He worked 4000 hours a week. His idea of relaxation on Sunday, after slaving until midnight all week in his store, was to place a big bet with Abe the bookie on a Sunday baseball game, a bet big enough to be painful if he lost, and then to watch the game on television and worry about it while doing the rent receipts for the buildings.

But he still had one problem: Affairs. *Bar mitzvahs* and weddings. He couldn't very well take his rent receipts to the affair. He couldn't go behind the bar and help the bartender. It wouldn't look right. So affairs presented a great problem to him. There was actually the danger that, for three hours every few months, he would be forced to relax and enjoy himself.

He solved this by volunteering to take home movies at every affair in our family. This was perfect for him. While everyone drank and danced, he could continue to work, to lug lights and extension cords around with him, to stay in harness, to maintain his authority ("Move a little to the left, Fanny. Now smile and dance with Lenny.") and to do a public service at the same time.

And the best part was that when relatives came over to visit us, he could show them movies. This meant he could work then, too, dealing with torn film, rewinding reels, and so on, and at the same time it meant he didn't have to talk to them.

Thus movie making was the perfect hobby for him. He pursued it at my *bar mitzvah* like any other occasion, training Burt to help out when he himself would have to be in the film.

But the film was not really what was worrying my father. You could see what was on his mind when the affair started and the guests began to eat the *hors d'oeuvres*. You could see he had figured out, over the past weeks, how much each individual *hors d'oeuvre* was costing him. It was, quite literally, as if they were eating his money itself.

To imagine his state of mind, think of all the years of not eating lunch, of walking five blocks to save a nickel on a parking meter, of driving three miles out of his way to avoid a toll of a quarter, and then imagine all this sacrifice, all those years of living on scrambled eggs morning and night while other people were eating in restaurants, and think of all these pennies and nickels saved, thousands of them, turned into dollar bills in a big bank vault, and then imagine all our relatives coming into the vault all dressed up, and sitting down, and eating his money while he had to stand there, smiling, and not saying a word.

This was how my father felt.

"Hello, Sid."

"Oh, hello, Faye. How are you?"

"Fine. This is a lovely affair. I love this liver knish."

My father smiled. "Wonderful. Enjoy yourself. Eat hearty. That's what it's there for."

A liver knish. Sixty-eight cents apiece! Thirty-four trips to Manny's candy store with a soda bottle he'd found in the street in order to get the two-cent deposit. Sixty-eight blocks of walking and she put it in her mouth just like that.

And now she was eating another one!

And she was not alone. There were dozens and dozens of them.

"Hi, Sid. Great affair."

"Thanks, Joe. I'm glad you like it."

Joe held up his glass. "J&B. Nothing but the best, Sid. First class."

"Thanks, Joe." (J&B. Even at wholesale, $4.95 a quart. Figure 25 big shots in a quart. 19.8¢ a shot.)

The waiter came by with a tray. Pigs in a blanket. Little hog dogs in baked dough. Joe took two. (2 x 39¢ = 78¢)

"Mmmm. These are delish. Have one, Sid."

"No thanks, Joe. I'm not hungry right now."

Joe took another. (39¢) Philly took two liver knishes. (2 x 68¢ = $1.36)

My father was feeling slightly ill. He could no longer even *see* the food. All he could see was dozens of people putting his life into their mouths. Sadie had just eaten his tip for walking three blocks in the snow the previous winter to deliver a fifth of Carstairs to two drunks in a fifth-floor walk-up. Oh, no, now she was putting that pair of underwear he needed but hadn't bought for himself down on Orchard Street into her mouth.

"Hiya, Sid. You're really doing yourself proud."

"Thanks, Howard."

My father tried to smile.

My mother, meanwhile, was having a grand time. She was in her glory, looking beautiful in her new red gown and following me around, basking in the praise offered to me by people who had heard me sing my *hoftorah* in the morning. People who knew I had always done well in school. They didn't know I was an apostate to the Jewish faith. They didn't know I had not only not read *Ivanhoe*, I had spent the last five school days hiding in the Hayden Planetarium, going on the "Trip to Venus" eighteen times.

I was feeling more and more guilty. I wanted to confess to everyone as they began to clear the room and to file upstairs for the supererogatory ceremony. Or at least they tried to get up the stairs. There seemed to be a temporary problem. It was my Cousin Dora from Brooklyn. All 300 pounds of her. She had gotten drunk and had fallen and gotten stuck on the stairs and she and the people who were attempting to free her up were blocking their way.

When everyone was seated in the synagogue, I stood with my parents in the vestibule behind the auditorium, still resisting as they made ready to walk down the aisle on the other side of the swinging doors.

"I can't do it, Dad. I just can't. I'm too embarrassed."

"You'll do it," he said quietly. "You'll do it or I'll break your goddamn neck."

"OK, go ahead," the manager, Nusserman, said to me. "Go ahead!" I could hear the cantor singing at the altar, but I couldn't move. "Go ahead!" Nusserman said again.

At this moment, the off-key soprano boomed into "Boy of Mine" from the balcony. She sounded like Kate Smith drowning. I lost control. I tried to make a run for it, heading for the exit to the street but my father grabbed me. He pulled me toward him, squeezing his fingers into my biceps until it felt like he had grabbed me right on the bones.

"I can't do it, Pop . . . That lady in the balcony . . . It's too much . . ."

"You'll go through it."

"I can't."

"I paid 100 bucks for this goddamn ceremony. I even paid twenty-five bucks for that goddamn soprano in the goddamn balcony. And you're gonna go through with this or I'll kill you." He released one arm, opened the swinging doors with his free hand, and with the other hand still on my bicep, he flung me down the aisle of the temple, and as I stumbled around trying to regain my balance, ("Boy of mine, boy of mine, I love him more each passing day . . .") as I looked up and saw more than a hundred pairs of eyes upon me, I began to walk down the aisle of the synagogue toward the altar and I heard people along the aisle whispering to each other, "If only his grandmother could have been alive to see this," and I heard women crying with heartfelt emotion.

116

Chapter 24

Somehow, we all survived my *bar mitzvah*. I was most pleased at the fact that my Aunt Rose had shown up. She had come out in public just to be there.

It was true she didn't look well. She looked broken, in fact. Still winsome in her way, but no longer in command of her health. More of her teeth were gone and she was very heavy, waddling around in a frilly little girl's dress, like a stuffed doll. But it was good to see her there. At dinner, after the extra ceremony, she called me to the table at which she was sitting, over in the corner, and she sang a purposely off-key version of "Boy of Mine," in her Eleanor Roosevelt falsetto. We both laughed together in a way we hadn't for some time.

After my *bar mitzvah*, my aunt returned to her life of secluded desuetude. Her decline could no longer be ignored. A family council was called. Bernie and Bessie went to talk to Rose along with my parents and Dr. Stern. Bernie was drunk, as he was almost every day during this period in which he was conducting an outrageous affair with Muriel Teitner and calling my father up in the middle of the night so they could insult each other.

Upon the doctor's advice, Rose began to see a psychiatrist. This was against her wishes, but she complied with the family's judgment and she went regularly with my mother accompanying her. This cost the family a great deal of money. It led to the psychiatrist recommending shock treatments for Rose. She was given these shock treatments, and others later, after the family decided it was in her best interests, and the best interests of the family, that she be helped before she deteriorated any further.

On one occasion Bernie and Bessie came over to our house after they had visited my aunt when she returned from the hospital. Bernie was fairly sober and the four of them were shaken by what was transpiring. They all loved Rose and it was not easy for them to put her through these shock treatments. I had been reading quietly in the living room. They ignored me although I could hear their conversation.

At one point, my father said, wearily, "Well, at least we can hope our kids will have better lives than this."

"Look, let's face it," Bernie said, "our kids will wind up just like we did. My Louie will be running my record store and your Danny will wind up in your liquor store."

"No I won't!" I said to myself. *"No I won't!"*

It was during this period that I began to have nightmares about an atomic attack on New York City. I would wake up sweating and chilled in the middle of the night, relieved to find that I had been dreaming, but despondent at the knowledge that there really was no escape from the insecurity which had invaded my waking life and which my dreams were shrieking about in the night.

I was studying hard in school now, and I had begun to think about college. I wanted out of The Bronx. I wanted a better life. But what was the point? What was the point of anything but immediate gratification when they were telling us on all sides—in the unsubtle language spoken by the presence of air raid drills and civil defense shelters—that everyone I loved and all that I was working for could be taken away from me in an instant by another maniac with a mustache in Europe.

One night I was jolted out of my sleep by a flash of lightning and a tremendous clash of thunder. I thought quickly, "Oh, no, this is it!" and stared into darkness while the windows rattled. But the world was still standing, and I fell back asleep. Next morning I padded across the street to speak to my Aunt Rose. She sat silently in her ancient house dress, at the window, looking at the wet street. It was the same window where she had taught me to read, using the newspapers, when I was four years old, puzzling out my first words:

NEW YORK DAILY NEWS.

I told Rose about my fears. At first she tried to change the subject by joking about my stuffy Aunt Evelyn, the wife of my Uncle Sol who owned a candy store in Brooklyn. Evelyn fancied herself the family social arbiter, a kind of Jewish Emily Post.

"Maybe we could threaten to drop your Aunt Evelyn on Russia if they start anything. That'd give them something to think about."

I couldn't help but smile.

"Do you remember that time, Danny, when you and Herbie were playing tag in your living room and she was sitting there on the couch like a queen? And you crawled over the arm and you wound up in her lap, and she squinched up her face and she started to swat your behind, back and forth with her hand, and then she said as she was swatting your backside, 'Feh! Feh! Get your ass out of my face. Feh! Feh!'"

We both laughed quietly. The room was dark. The rain had stopped but the sky was still overcast and ominous. As my aunt laughed, I was struck by her fragility. In spite of her excess weight, her laughter was somehow rusty sounding and small. As she lit up a cigarette, I noticed how few teeth she had left.

"And remember your mother came in and Evelyn said (Rose began to imitate Evelyn's voice and expression perfectly), 'Wait a minute, boys. Danny, and you, too, Herbie, you *bonditt*, let me tell you something, and Ceil will be my witness. You boys've never been in society, but Ceil, when you go into society, is it right, I mean is it *ever* proper to put your ass in another person's face? Tell them, Ceil, is it ever proper in society to even put your ass *near* another person's face?'"

Rose sat there, rocking in the dun light and giggling at the vast mad painful comedy in which she had found herself for all these years. Then she looked up at me and said, softly, serious now, "But I'm not helping you, am I kid?"

"It's OK, Aunt Rose."

Now I was sorry I had brought up the matter of the bomb and my nightmares and fears because suddenly I realized, for the first time, that although Rose was my aunt and an adult, and I was just a kid, she needed help more than I did.

But this time she purposely moved the conversation back to the bomb.

"It scares you, don't it kid?"

I nodded yes.

"What are you afraid of?"

"Everything."

"Everything?"

"Yeah, that it'll blow up everything. And everything'll be ruined, like those pictures they show on TV of all those bombed down cities in the war. And I won't get to go to college or to grow up or anything."

We sat there, breathing the moist, still air.

"Is there any one thing you think of?" she said. "Is there really one thing on your mind the most?"

I swallowed. Hesitated. Then spoke: "Yeah."

"What is it? . . . What is it, Danny?"

"That it'll kill my father," I said. "I'm afraid they'll drop a bomb and we'll be OK, and it'll kill my father."

We sat there together, looking at the floor. It began to drizzle outside. We listened to the rain. Then my aunt said, quietly, "Well, I don't know much about bombs, Danny. So maybe you asked the wrong person. But for what it's worth, I'll tell you one thing I think. I don't think God put us all here, and had us suffer all this stupidity and pain and all this ignorance all around us, just to blow us all up someday. I really don't."

When I didn't answer, she added, quietly, "I really don't think God put us here for nothing . . . But I'll tell you another thing, Danny, and this is the truth, I don't have the foggiest idea of why he did put us here."

We sat there together in silence. I don't know for how long. Then I left, walking slowly outside into the soft rain.

Chapter **25**

My Uncle Lenny bought them. The General Eisenhower ties. They were maroon with three pictures of General Eisenhower on them and under each, "I LIKE IKE." He gave me one and I wore it often.

Most of the people in our neighborhood were backing Ike as opposed to Adlai Stevenson. Ike had "taken care of our boys" in World War Two and he would take care of us now. He had stood up to Hitler and he would stand up to Joe Stalin.

Stevenson was hurt by his image as an intellectual. To most people on the block, this meant he was "out of it." A nice guy, a great college president, but they felt a thug like Joe Stalin would make mincemeat out of him.

In that fall of 1952, I started at De Witt Clinton High School. Clinton's main attraction was its reputation as a pretty tough school. We had only three possible grades at the end of the semester: A, D, or M.I.A. A meant alive. If you went to school all year and emerged alive in June you got an A. If you didn't emerge alive, you got a D for dead. If you left for school one morning and were never heard from again but nobody found the body you got an M.I.A., for missing in action.

OK, I'm kidding. I admit it. But Clinton *was* a tough school. That was part of its charm for me. 3500 boys. No girls. The school district included the entire Bronx and Harlem. The school had a reputation throughout New York for being tough and for having good teams in all sports, but it was also known as a place where you could get a good education. It had many famous alumni. Not only professional sports greats such as Dolph Schayes and many others, but writers, too. From that single high school graduated Nathaniel West, Henry Roth, James Baldwin, Paddy Chayefsky, Bruce Jay Friedman, and Neil Simon.

But I didn't know this at the time. What attracted me was Clinton's image which conjoined a kind of boys' prep school with a blackboard jungle madhouse. On the one hand, the school was outside of our neighborhood, in the North Bronx, at the edge of a park. It sprawled in a lovely verdant setting, alongside ample athletic fields: a handsome large, three-story building with ivied walls and inner courtyards containing formal gardens. This landscape and its sports traditions conflated in my mind to become the light and dark blue of Clarkston Prep from my boys' books.

On the other hand, it was filled with guys from Harlem and from parts of The Bronx which you didn't enter without the National Guard behind you. It was not exactly Hometown High in Midwest, U.S.A. For example, we had a student organization called the G.O. which collected fifty cents from each kid each semester. For this you would get a G.O. card which admitted you into the old Madison Square Garden at a discount so you could see ⅔ of a basketball game. I say ⅔ because although you could stay for the entire game, from the seats they gave us in the side balcony, you could only see ⅔ of the court. And that was standing up. If you sat down, you got to see ½ a game.

In my junior year, after the G.O. had sold 3000 cards, some students broke into the school at night, *dynamited* the G.O. safe, and took the money. It was as simple as that. Nothing sophisticated. Just blow the shit out of the whole G.O. office and take the money. That was Clinton.

But it was romantic to me. I wanted to go to school with desperadoes from the East Bronx. I wanted to meet black guys from Harlem. I wanted to get out of my neighborhood and into what I saw as a world of larger possibilities, of openings to adventure, for better or for worse. I wanted something beyond Doris Day singing, "Secret Love," Pattie Page's "Doggie in the Window," and Eddie Fisher's, "Oh My Papa, to me he was so wonderful."

And, to tell you the truth, I didn't mind the fact that Clinton wasn't co-ed either. You see, things were not going smoothly between the boys and the girls in The Bronx at this time in my life. Especially for me. I was not the best-looking guy to grace the world. I was so fat I could have been an inflated float in the Macy's Parade. As my Cousin Herbie used to say, when God said all those who want good looks come forth, I came fifth.

The girls hadn't liked me that much in junior high. They preferred handsome shallow boys like Marshall Larkin. I spent my time with unpopular boys like Eugene Feldstein who got 98 on every exam. Eugene had earned an official "expert" ranking in chess. He played matches by mail with adults from around the world. I liked Eugene. He had figured out a diet that was nutritionally perfect, so he ate the same food every day. He and I used to take the subway to a chess club near Fourteenth Street where I was able to see world-class masters including Edward Lasker play.

Meanwhile, boys like Marshall Larkin spent their time at the mirror, combing their hair and preparing themselves to be God's gift to women. And when it came time to vote for best athlete, Marshall won. Most girls in the class voted for him. Marshall Larkin! The best athlete! If you had told him to "hit and run" he probably would have driven over someone in a car.

Boys and girls had been raised pretty much separately in our neighborhood. We were like two universes, matter and anti-matter, which existed in the same space but were largely invisible to each other. For example, although my Cousin Louie was one of my closest friends, his sister Carol, who was only a few months younger than I, was hardly an intimate acquaintance at all. I mean, we *liked* each other. We liked each other a great deal, in fact. But we never really sat down and talked together. We had different interests and friends and we seemed to operate in different worlds.

And this was true for most boys and girls in The Bronx at this time. If we had a Halloween party, everyone would be awkward in relating to each other. The girls would be fastidiously polite while some boy like Herbie would show up in a skeleton costume and would run around on the furniture with his shoes. Clowning seemed much easier than talking to girls. What would we talk about? They seemed so different.

If we had a pre-teen dance, say in the casino at Ha-Ya Bungalows, the girls would dance the Lindy with each other while the boys would sit around and say, "I'll dance, right? When they come out and play baseball, I'll dance." Of course, the idea of girls playing baseball seemed about as likely as Senator Joe McCarthy going on the road with the Count Basie Band.

This was an unfortunate situation. We all lost from this sexual stereotyping. And when we approached puberty in junior high school, the inexperience and distance between us surfaced with a vengeance. No one knew how to handle the new juices which were forcing themselves through our bodies, and we all acted a little crazy. Somehow, having girls around caused the boys to turn everything they did into a performance. In sports, for example, what had once been a team effort became a branch of show business. I imagine it was similar for the girls. So I wasn't sorry to go to De Witt Clinton, where relationships between the boys weren't warped by the need they felt to show off for the girls.

And puberty! Puberty hit The Bronx like Hurricane Yetta. On the good side, within two years, I grew nine inches and hardly gained a pound. I had stopped eating as much once I left home and centered my life around my new friends at high school and around the Philadelphians' games in the neighborhood. Suddenly I found myself a gangling stork of a boy, six feet tall and 160 pounds. No more would I put in two hook shots in a row from the foul line and hear a guy yell to his friend, "Hey, Howie! Come over here fast and look at this fat guy play!"

And there was no oil shortage in The Bronx in those days. I felt as if I had enough oil on my skin alone to light the entire city of Schenectady, New York, for several weeks. My face broke out so badly that for a while I was ashamed to go out of the house in the daylight. After school, I would stay at home and read until the sun went down, and only then would I venture out to the schoolyard to shoot jumpshots by myself in the weak light from the windows of a large apartment house which rose alongside the court.

One day my father took me aside. From the way he wasn't looking directly into my eyes, I knew I was in for a "man-to-man" talk.

"Don't you want to have nice skin, Danny?"

"Sure, Dad."

"Then don't you know what to do?"

124

"Do?"

"Yeah. Don't you know how to cure your pimples?"

"Cure them?"

"Yeah. Cure them. Just stop doing it."

"Doing it?"

"Yeah."

"Doing what?"

"You know . . ."

"No, I don't."

"You really don't?"

"No."

"Stop abusing yourself."

"Abusing myself?"

"Yeah. Stop abusing yourself."

"What's 'Abusing yourself'?"

"Don't you know what's 'Abusing yourself'?"

"No."

"You really don't know?"

"No, Dad. I don't know."

"Stop jerking off," he said.

"But, Dad, I don't jerk off."

"You don't?"

"No, Dad. I swear. I don't."

"Well, stop it anyhow," he said, and he quickly walked away.

Later that month, I jerked off for the first time.

Chapter **26**

One of the first friends I made at De Witt Clinton was a black guy named La Rue Johnston. We met on the Lexington Avenue El on the first day of school. The train came up through Harlem, picking up all the black guys, and then through The Bronx, heading north, fetching the rest of us. We Philadelphians gathered each morning, walked the quarter of a mile to the station together, and then rode up to school, meeting our friends from Harlem on the train. By the time the train had reached Kingsbridge Road, virtually everyone remaining on it either attended Clinton, or Walton, the girls' school nearby.

The Philadelphians were all on the train that first day when, at Kingsbridge Road, La Rue had his head out the door, jiving with some of the black girls who had just gotten off to go to Walton. The door on this old I.R.T. subway car emerged from just one side of the frame and traveled all the way across the doorway. A six-inch-wide slab of hard rubber at the end bounced anyone it hit out of the way. On this particular morning, the rubber edge of the door caught La Rue right on the neck, and somehow it clicked closed with his head still in it, sticking out of the train. Unbelievably, the train started to move. We were all momentarily frozen into inaction by this extraordinary. occurrence. Even La Rue's friend, Ernie Jones. We could not conceive of the train continuing to move with La Rue's head stuck in the door, but it did. Finally, Ernie panicked and began yelling, "Stop the train!" As everyone scurried about looking for the emergency brake, my Cousin Louie leaped up, grabbed La Rue around the waist, put both his feet up against the door, and PUSHED, and there was an odd PLOP sound as La Rue's head popped out of the door, and he and Louie shot backwards across the car, La Rue landing on top of Louie on the floor.

This wasn't the most ordinary way to make friends or to begin a high school career, but when everyone had finally stopped laughing hysterically, we introduced ourselves. From that day on La Rue and Ernie were special friends with the Philadelphians.

The train rides to Clinton, and especially *from* Clinton in the afternoons, were always special events. One afternoon my Cousin Herbie and I left school late. The car was empty until we got to Walton, where the station was loaded with girls. "Watch this," Herbie said, stretching out on the seats which ran along the side of the car. He thought in his wise guy way that taking up four seats would give him a chance to meet the girls when they asked him if they might sit down. When the train came to a stop, however, and the girls came pouring on by the dozens, four big girls just picked him up without a word and threw him on the floor.

The morons thought it was great fun on the way home to throw the train's light bulbs out the windows. The I.R.T. subway cars had bare light bulbs in sockets in the ceilings. By simply standing on the seat you could unscrew them and then throw them out the windows of the El onto the people below. And best of all, they exploded when they hit the ground.

This was fun for the morons for a while, but when they realized the seat cushions were also removable, they escalated the stakes involved. The cushions were steel on the bottom with a woven straw top over the metal springs inside. They were heavy and could be dangerous. So someone got the bright idea of throwing *them* out of the windows one day when all the light bulbs were gone. Then someone got another bright idea: Since there were trackwalkers along the old El, men who were paid to inspect the rails and signals and so forth, and these trackwalkers would get over to the side, adjacent to the low railing on the El structure when a train passed by, the game involved throwing a seat cushion out of the window in an attempt to knock the trackwalker off the El structure so he would fall to the street below.

You could always tell when "Clinton men" were on the train after school. They would break into the motormen's compartments which were in each car, and blow the whistles madly, so as the train pulled into a station, whistles would be blowing and seats flying out of the windows along with light bulbs that were exploding.

Life inside the school wasn't much saner. One day when I arrived at school late, the halls were empty of students except for one guy, Vinnie Tamburo. The two deans had him against the wall, pinning him there by his shoulders, while the principal shouted at him, "Don't give me that! I heard you say, 'Let's attack Walton!'" The principal worked him over with a series of lefts and rights to the mid-section as the deans held him helpless against the wall.

The sun never rose on a quiet day at De Witt Clinton. Several huge mooks who had been going there for years had come to seem like permanent fixtures in the building. Older than everyone else, some of them were among the handful of guys who owned cars. They would come to school most often in the winter, perhaps because the school was warmer than their apartments.

Each of them had a gang of followers. When they did show up on warm days, they terrorized the vendors who sold ice cream out of trucks on the street during the lunch periods. One day, Sol Patinsky, one of these huge mooks, approached a new ice cream vendor. Sol explained who he was and that he and his boys got a free ice cream pop every day. The vendor was small but brazen. He replied, "I don't know you or your boys. You can take your pop and shove it." At this, two of the "boys" grabbed the vendor and held him while Solly opened up the hood of his truck and began to rip out wires as if he were cleaning a chicken. When the vendor showed up again the next week, he gave Solly and his boys their pops without saying a word except, "Pistachio or vanilla?"

One spring, two new vendors showed up at once, a Bungalow Bar and a Good Humor man. They parleyed together and decided they wouldn't give in to the big mooks but would take a determined stand and resist. On the next day six guys held them while Solly and his boys took the brake off the Good Humor truck. Val Parducci and his boys did the same with the Bungalow Bar. They pushed the trucks a half a block away from each other, they got as many guys as could fit behind each truck, and they ran them toward each other as fast as they could, smashing them into each other head on. They then separated the trucks, gave out all the ice cream, and turned the trucks over on their sides, leaving them lying there in the gutter.

These same guys, Val and Solly and several others, decided once in a while that it was time for a holiday. They stood outside the El station and when we emerged they would shout, "St. Paramount's Day!" We'd all turn around en masse, go back onto the station, and travel down to Times Square where we caught the early show at the Paramount. This became a kind of school tradition and we eagerly awaited it.

Many students cut school every day. The authorities couldn't do much about it. Once you were inside the building, however, they made every effort to keep you there. As you might imagine, De Witt Clinton usually had a good football team. Even if they didn't win, they would send several of their opponents to the hospital. Not even spectators were safe at the games. There was a legend that once, on the way to the big game against Stuyvesant on Randall's Island, a group of the big mooks and their boys had taken chains and had hung some poor guy off the bridge over the East River until the police came.

During school hours the football team would practice by taking positions on the large lawn in the park between the school and the El station. If you ran out of the school and tried to make it to the El, they would tackle you and bring you back. My Cousin Herbie tried to escape via this route a few times. He did do some nice broken field running, but each time someone finally brought him down and the other guys piled on and they sort of beat the shit out of him.

Before the Stuyvesant game we would always have a football assembly. The entire team, 86 guys, squeezed on the stage in full uniform, the Clinton band, the coach, and thousands of maniacs all giving the school cheer:

Give 'em the ax the ax the ax
Give 'em the ax the ax the ax
Where? Where?
Right in the neck.

And they would bring "Prof" Waldman out on the stage. Prof was a kind of school totem. He was an old guy who had had polio so he could hardly walk, a terrific, crusty old guy, and he would somehow make it across the stage on his crutches, while everyone would be going totally berserk, cheering and screaming. Prof had been at the school for approximately ninety years. He *was* De Witt Clinton. He directed the school honor society in which I ran a tutorial program: the better students helped the poorer students. So we always got along fine and I liked him. Prof would come out and give the student body his pep talk, and the sight of this crippled old guy telling the boys on the team to win for old "De Witt C," drove everyone wild. It was as if the Stuyvesant guys weren't just playing a football game. It was as if they were beating up on old Prof himself, a courageous but finally helpless cripple.

It moved the students to the edge of madness. In one instance, someone handed Prof a football and at the height of the crowd's emotion, he tossed it right in the midst of the 86 players and yelled, "Fumble!" and they all piled on as we cheered like mad, and then they peeled off leaving the one guy who had been on the bottom totally unconscious and almost suffocated. They had to take the guy to the hospital where he recovered quickly with just two broken ribs, but he missed the big game.

When we played an away game with a co-ed school like Evander Childs, the authorities on both sides were always near panic. Clinton men had a reputation for being crazy with women and whether it was true or not many of the boys felt an obligation to live up to it. At Evander, there were two separate grandstands, one on each side of the field. The Evander stand was protected by an eight-foot-high fence. When you arrived at the game you had to show your G.O. card and you were forced to sit on your school's side of the field.

To the Clinton guys, this was maddening. There, barely fifty yards away on the other side of the field, were GIRLS. All the "Romeos" on the Clinton side were certain the girls were dying to meet them. So who could blame them when, during the half-time intermission, they all lined up in a single row of hundreds of guys down the center of the field from goal post to goal post. Augie Metaxa played a cavalry charge on his trumpet and they rushed the Evander stands in a human wave. The principal of our school, and the deans, and the gym teachers, had anticipated something like this, however, and they had formed a defensive line in front of the stands. As the human wave arrived they began to punch out kids and to pull guys down off the fence left and right, but there were too many students. They could only hit and pull down dozens, while there were hundreds involved in the charge.

Nothing much ever happened with the girls in the second half. But one could always count on a good number of fights in the stands which made the game interesting even if the score was lopsided.

Our home basketball games were equally insane. If the referee made a bad call against us in a crucial situation, everyone would run out of the gym into the parking lot and turn the ref's car upside down.

I was beginning to like school at last.

But why was it that the kindling of a riot or a fight or the wrecking of a train would not fail to send an undeniable *frisson* of delicious illicit pleasure up my spine? Was it that I had been so constrained in a jail of the spirit circumscribed by my father's violence and my mother's social ambitions that the vital force within me thrilled at any chance to identify with "the children" when they destroyed the property and flouted the laws of "the adults"? Had I been so victimized by violence that my terror at its inception turned to coursing delight whenever I saw it was directed at someone other than myself? And did I enjoy seeing two rigid, self-certain, dudes slugging it out in the service of some violent male ethos because on some unconscious level they reminded me of younger versions of my father, finally getting their comeuppance from someone their own size?

If, as the students of child abuse say, "Victims breed victims," that is, child abusers were often abused themselves, why didn't I turn victimizer when I grew older? Was there something in my nature or upbringing, something cowardly or perhaps fine, that had always led me to recoil from actual participation in violence, however much I might have enjoyed watching it when I was young? Or was my joy and vicarious participation in violence the fire which burned the impotent fury within me into white ash that finally fell away, softly, on its own.

And at the social level, is there enough wit extant at present to deal with the Hitlers on every level of society without recourse, at some point, to some form of violence?

Chapter 27

Sometimes, after school, on a day when the Yankees were playing a night game, I would remain on the train for two additional stops, journeying to Yankee Stadium to talk to the players as they arrived. This always seemed unbelievable to me: that you could, simply by loitering outside the stadium, get to talk to the players—Mickey Mantle, Whitey Ford, Billy Martin. The same players whom the men at Ha-Ya Bungalows discussed for hours. The same players who appeared on TV and in the newspapers every day, the players thousands of people paid money to see at a distance. You could walk with them and talk to them for free.

It was like getting in touch with Real Life.

Of course, things didn't always go smoothly. One afternoon I ran over to greet Yankee pitcher Allie Reynolds, called "The Big Chief." I had seen so many photos of him, had watched him pitch so many times, that he seemed like an old friend. I ran right up to him and said, "Whaddya say, Big Chief?" I expected a warm response. He grunted and shoved me roughly out of the way. Well, perhaps he'd had a hard day. For all I knew maybe he blamed me for stealing this country from his people three hundred years ago. If the kids at Sacred Heart School could spit on us for "killing the Savior" when the Philadelphians played basketball in their gym, anything was possible.

This spitting on basketball players was always an inconvenience, especially if you played games in the South Bronx or Harlem. After a while we avoided playing in gyms with running tracks above the court. The fans up there let you have it throughout the game, and this made it difficult to enjoy what you were doing.

We had our own gym for home games in P.S. 73 on Anderson Avenue. Pop Goldman had reserved it for us. Pop continued to meet with us each month, and through his guidance and leadership we stayed together as a club, buying various uniforms, and reversible maroon and gold jackets. He really helped us out, Pop did, and we all respected him, but the jackets got us into trouble. We first heard about it via tremors on the invisible reticule of urban rumor: a gang called the Bronx Counts were after us. They claimed we had stolen their colors.

The Bronx Counts were tough. Once we had played them in football when one of their linemen broke his leg on the first play. As he lay there on the ground in agony, we asked the Counts' leader what we should do. "Cover him up with a blanket and we'll play around him."

Fortunately, he was only kidding. Their leader was a madman named Victor Dubinsky. He was one of the toughest guys in Taft High School. Even the Mad German didn't mess with him. The word on the street was that he was extremely upset about our stealing their colors and that when he caught up with us he was going to kill us. We assumed there was some hyperbole involved in this statement, but with Victor you couldn't be 100% sure.

One night, after a game against the Sedgwick Eagles, five of us stayed late at P.S. 73 to shoot baskets until the school closed. There was Skinny Diamond, Midge Waxenthal, Huge Marvin, Herbie and myself. As we walked home along dark, totally deserted Woodycrest Avenue, three guys appeared from behind a car. Bronx Counts! Victor Dubinsky and two other vicious morons.

"Hold it right there, jerks," Victor said.

We held it right there.

"Get against the wall, motherfuckers."

"What's this all about?" Herbie said.

I began to get worried about what Herbie might say. He had been acting a little crazy lately. Only the week before he had walked up to a Puerto Rican couple on 170th Street and had kissed the girl. The guy hit him over the head with a bottle. Six stitches at Morrisainia Hospital were necessary to close the gash.

"You mean there's three of us and five of you guys?" Victor said with an evil leer.

"Yeah, I guess you could say that," Herbie said.

"Well, motherfucker, you're wrong." Victor pulled out a gun. The barrel shone dark gray and hideous in the dull street light. The handle was wood.

"OK, Victor, take it easy," Midge said.

"Let's get against the wall like he says," Huge Marvin said to Herbie.

We lined up against the wall. Victor had the pistol at his hip.

"I see you guys stole our fuckin' colors."

"What colors?" I said.

"My mother's colors, you jerk." He pointed the gun at my face.

"Oh, you mean the colors of our jackets," I said.

"Oh, you mean the colors of our jackets," the heavier of the two morons with Victor said in a high-pitched voice, mimicking me.

"Look, enough of this shit," Victor said. "Let's just kill them."

"Kill us?" Midge said.

"Kill all of us?" Skinny said.

"Whaddya say, boys. Should we kill them all?" Victor said.

The heavy guy said, "Why waste the bullets? Let's just kill one of them."

"Yeah," the other one said. "If we kill one of them, they'll never wear those fuckin' jackets again."

"OK," Victor said, smiling. "But which one should we kill?"

"Why not shoot the biggest one?" the heavy guy said.

"Yeah, shoot the biggest one," the other guy said.

Well, once we heard that "shoot the biggest one," 80% of us breathed easier. I was six feet tall, Herbie was five foot nine, Skinny was five foot eight, Midge was five foot five and Huge Marvin was over six foot five. I remember thinking to myself with great relief, "Oh, thank you, God. They're only going to shoot Marvin."

Then the strangest thing happened, an occurrence shrouded in mystery which was to become a neighborhood legend never to be satisfactorily explained. We all looked up at Huge Marvin, but when we did, he wasn't there. I mean he *was* there, but he wasn't *up* there where he was supposed to be, a half a foot higher than the rest of us, ready to be killed.

No, Marvin was there, with this terrified expression on his face,

134

but he was so frightened and hunched up, that he was *compressed*. Unbelievably, Huge Marvin was suddenly no bigger than the rest of us. Somehow, by sheer force of will, in that critical moment, Marvin seemed to have shrunk to normal size.

At this point, we *all* panicked. But then, again unbelievably, my cousin Herbie said, "I bet that's not even a real gun."

We all looked at the gun and it did have a home-made look to it, with an improvised wooden handle.

"Oh, no?" Victor said. "You insulting me? I made this piece myself."

"You see?" Herbie said. "I told you it wasn't real."

"NOT REAL?" Victor shouted. "It's a fuckin' zip gun you asshole!" He pointed the gun toward Herbie's head, raised it slightly, and fired. BOOM. The bullet whacked against the brick wall, inches over Herbie's head, and with bright, frightening sparks, ricocheted across the street.

Herbie turned absolutely white. People began to switch on their lights and open their windows in the large apartment houses around us. The heavy guy said to Victor, "Shit, let's get outa here." As they trotted down the street, Victor turned and shouted over his shoulder, "It's real, motherfucker! I let you off this time. Next time it's forever."

We never again wore our jackets on Woodycrest Avenue at night.

Chapter 28

At first I thought that intelligence might be a handicap at De Witt Clinton. Then I found that being one of the smartest kids could be an asset as long as you didn't mind when a big mook copied from you on an exam. In fact, if you would go out of your way to let the mook know you didn't mind, you would gain protection from him and his boys.

My friend La Rue was in my algebra class. La Rue was bright enough in most of his courses, but he simply didn't have a sense of math. His friend Ernie would help him at home, and I helped him by staying after school to work with him on the days before exams. Between us we got him through. (Later, when I had become a modern jazz fanatic, La Rue paid me back by taking me to the Apollo Theater in Harlem several times. Once I realized how friendly the people there were to me, I began to go back on my own, but it was La Rue who introduced me to the Apollo as well as to Dexter Holmes, an ex-jazz musician who owned a record store in Harlem. Dexter took a liking to me and spent many afternoons when business was slow initiating me into the mysteries of jazz chord changes.)

Passing algebra was important to La Rue because he had made the basketball team and had to keep up his grades to qualify. I nearly made the team, but I was cut on the final day. My last tryout was a little strange. The coach, "Crazy Abe" Jablonski, thought it would be amusing to put me up against the school's all-city center, a guy from Harlem named Elmer "Louisiana" Williams who was six foot nine.

Well, as I said, I didn't make the team.

Coach Jablonski was called "Crazy Abe" and was a legendary institution at Clinton. Built like a barrel, he was robust and tough. He never went anywhere without a huge chair leg he carried with him. It was menacing, dark and heavy. It looked like a drumstick from a giant turkey.

"Crazy Abe" was one of the few people at the school who could maintain discipline. The most difficult time for the teachers was during the lunch periods. Besides the usual scuffles and mini-riots occurring in the normal course of 1000 urban boys from different races and ethnic backgrounds hanging around together in an unstructured situation, sometimes organized brawls broke out. We'd hear the word in the morning: "Blacks against the Italians on the basketball court outside at noon." At noon, we'd all go out to watch as 100 black guys and 100 Italians would line up at opposite ends of the courts. Of course, if all the students in the school had heard about this, the authorities had too, and at this point police cars usually came flying around the building and everyone ran like hell.

But if the police didn't get there in time, the school's next line of defense was "Crazy Abe." In these instances, "Crazy Abe" would come barrelling around the building yelling like a wildman, brandishing his chair leg like a hatchet. In reality, even "Crazy Abe" was no match for 1000 boys, but over the years the boys had learned something very interesting—they had learned that it was more fun and almost as dangerous to run as a mob from "Crazy Abe" than it was to have the fight itself.

When one of the boys saw "Crazy Abe" steaming around the corner, he would shout, "Crazy Abe!" Everyone would join in, shouting, "Crazy Abe!" as if they were terrified. Everyone would flee in feigned panic toward the entrance to the school where they would all try to thrust themselves through the doors at once. The boys loved it. You could squash people, trample people, crush people, step on people, and it was all "Good fun," no meanness attached. It was like some great sport, all of us running toward the building at once in a mad rush with "Crazy Abe" behind us, jamming us into the doorway together, and as people fell and were trampled and stomped on, "Crazy Abe" raged at our backs, herding us in by beating wildly on the boys at the edge of the mob with his shillelagh.

A charge by "Crazy Abe" was by far the most exciting part of any day at school.

After school I continued to see more of my Uncle Lenny than my father. Lenny and Aunt Fanny felt guilty about the fact that Herbie was an only child. Since they thought this might be the reason why he behaved erratically at times and was often depressed, they usually took me along when they went out as a family. One restaurant they went to was called "Mike's Ship Ahoy," near the old St. Nicholas Arena in Manhattan. The food wasn't exceptionally good, but my uncle and aunt liked it because there were about twenty boats on the floor of the restaurant and each table was situated in its own little ship.

When we first went there, my uncle turned to the waiter and called across the room, "Gar-Kahn! Gar-Kahn!"

"Gar-Kahn?" Herbie said.

"It means 'waiter' in French," my uncle said, proudly.

Lenny would take us to games. One memorable incident occurred at a football game on a rainy afternoon. It was a Yankee football game, when they and the Dodgers had teams in the old All-America Conference.

After the game we went down on the playing surface to cut across the field, running imaginary plays with each other on the way out. It had stopped drizzling. Some kids from Harlem tore down the goal posts. They broke them up into large weapons and proceeded to gambol about the field beating people with them. When one of them approached us, my uncle stepped forward, pulled out his umbrella, assumed a dueling stance, and began fencing in the air in front of the guy, while shouting, "Lunge! Lunge!" Well, seeing this bald ex-wrestler type yelling, "Lunge! Lunge!" must have freaked the guy with the five foot chunk of goal post, because he immediately stopped in this tracks, turned around, and decided to hit somebody else.

On the way home, we congratulated my uncle on his tremendous if zany courage and he beamed with pride. "It was nothing, boys. That's why it pays, though, to study the marital arts."

"The marital arts?" I said.

"Yeah . . . You know . . . Fighting."

He was a great guy, my uncle. He coached the Philadelphians when we won The Bronx Championship in *The New York Mirror*-Department of Parks Basketball Tournament. Although we had Huge Marvin and my Cousin Louie who was formidable off the boards for his size, we knew we needed another big man up front. So we enlisted a ringer—La Rue Johnston. La Rue was not eligible to play in the tournament because he was technically a member of the Clinton team. Like most sophomores, however, he was virtually never put into a game. Few would recognize him as a high school varsity athlete, but we couldn't take any chances. We had to get him a birth certificate so he could play under an assumed name.

It was not easy to get a birth certificate for La Rue. Everyone we asked was reluctant to donate an official paper to someone from Harlem who might then be shown in photos in *The New York Mirror* and identified by the name of the donor. Finally we approached one boy who didn't play ball at all but who yearned for our acceptance. Fortunately, he agreed to loan La Rue his birth certificate. Unfortunately, his name was Israel Moscowitz. When the Department of Parks official checked us in for the first game, La Rue handed him the birth certificate. The man looked up at La Rue, who was black as coal, and said, incredulously, *"You're* Israel Moscowitz?"

"That's right, boss," La Rue said.

The man finally just shrugged his shoulders and checked Israel's name on the approved list. We had great fun after that, calling La Rue, "Izzy," on the way to school on the train in the mornings. Sometimes Louie even did it during the games. When he wanted La Rue to pass him the ball, he'd yell, "Izzy! Over here, Izzy!"

It wasn't unusual to use a ringer in this tournament. Most of the good teams had a player or two in the same position as La Rue. As I said, we did well in the tournament, and we found ourselves within one game of playing in Madison Square Garden. We had to play the Manhattan champs at Mullaly Gym in The Bronx. The winner would play the Brooklyn-Queens winner in the Garden. My Uncle Lenny was wild with enthusiasm. He seemed to cherish the idea of coaching in the Garden as much as we looked forward to the possibility of playing there. When the big day came, my uncle rounded up half the neighborhood to root for us. He was nervously optimistic until the Manhattan champs came out onto the court. They were huge. La Rue recognized some of them from Harlem. It turned out they had *four* ringers, two from Commerce High and two from Ben Franklin. We couldn't protest since we were guilty of the same infraction of the rules.

We actually shot better than they did, but it seemed that they got four shots to our one and they beat us by twelve points.

After the game, when our fans from the neighborhood stopped by the dressing room to console us, my uncle kept repeating, "All my boys saw was shoes out there. You can't blame my boys. They can't be expected to play against leapers like that. All my boys saw were shoes."

Then, about two months later, tragedy struck. One of the two great tragedies of my high school years. My Uncle Lenny made *The Daily News* for the third time:

EX-HERO NABBED
IN D.C. HEIST

It was my Uncle Lenny. Now we finally learned where he had been getting his money all these years. He had been the leader of a gang of five black men. All six had tommy guns. They had been holding up banks in the Washington D.C.–Baltimore area for years. Now they had tried to hold up a Washington night club. Along with the women's jewelry they also had taken the men's pants, apparently figuring that by this means they would get all the valuables and that the men would be hesitant to pursue them. They didn't realize there was a telephone in the back of the kitchen. A cook, who had been in the bathroom, stealthily moved over and called the police before crawling out a back window.

The police surrounded the club. There was some gunfire, and a policeman was wounded before my Uncle Lenny and his boys were forced to surrender in the face of overwhelming odds.

Thus my uncle, who had become a hero by helping Tiny Nizell sit on the guy who robbed Daitch's Dairy; who had made the papers a second time when he fell into the I.R.T. while taking us swimming, now made *The Daily News* a third time. There was a large photo of him in the paper, along with photos of President Eisenhower and John Foster Dulles.

They put my uncle in the federal penitentiary in Maryland. When they checked his records, they found two previous convictions for armed robberies when he was a young man. No one in the family had known about this. My uncle knew they would throw the book at him—one white man, a third offender, leading five black men with tommy guns in committing federal offenses and shooting an officer when they were caught.

He expected to get twenty-five years to life.

I never saw him again. I would have gone all the way to Maryland to see him but I wasn't able to. He wouldn't see anyone but my Aunt Fanny and Herbie. He wouldn't even see my father. His shame was too great.

Three months after he was arrested, he cut his wrists in his cell and he died.

I missed my uncle very much after he was gone. I didn't care whether he robbed banks or not. He was always loving and generous to me.

Chapter 29

During the spring of his last year of high school, my Cousin Herbie began to read the existentialists. Camus, Sartre, Heidegger, Nietzsche—he read them all, day and night, and the more he read, the more depressed he seemed to get.

On one occasion, he was sitting on the stoop with such a troubled look on his face that I walked over to ask him what was wrong.

"I don't know. I'm reading this guy Celine. He's unbelievable."

"In what way? Is he like Camus?"

"This guy influenced Camus. He's totally nuts, Danny. I mean really wacko. It's so depressing I can't believe it."

"So why continue with it?"

"I don't know . . . Sometimes what he says seems so true to me . . . Sometimes I can't bear it . . ."

"Well, Jesus, Herbie, put the book down for a while."

"Not the book, Danny. The world."

He isolated himself by this reading. He was over a year older than I and two important years ahead of me in school. There was no one else he could talk to. I mean, in our neighborhood, to say no one else read the existentialists at that time would be quite an understatement. They wouldn't have recognized an existentialist if one of them had come up and bit them on the street.

Somehow, he also learned about Yoga. He took to doing his *asanas* in the street, sitting cross-legged or standing on his head on the sidewalk. He got beaten up a couple times for doing this. I guess people felt he was showing off, or giving the block a bad name. Maybe they thought Yoga was un-American.

Once, after he had graduated from high school, he decided with Lobo Fox to attempt to play chess in the Blarney Stone Tavern on Plimpton Avenue. This quickly set the regular patrons into action. They ran over to the table, picked up Herbie, Lobo, their chairs, and the chess set, and threw them all out into the street.

I was making my own forays into the realm of culture during my high school years. I was looking for a broader, deeper, more satisfying world, but, as with my reading adventures, beginning wasn't easy. For example, I wanted to hear classical music. I had always heard of this thing called classical music and I wanted to check it out. But where did one begin? Well, the obvious place was Carnegie Hall. So I watched the newspapers. One night I put on a suit and tie, so much Vitalis on my hair that it ran into my eye, and set out for the concert, on the subway, by myself.

I went to hear Mantovani. I imagined this was the best that the world of serious music had to offer. Carnegie Hall was filled. I sat in the last row. When the maestro concluded with his famous "Greensleeves," everyone broke into extended applause and I joined in, feeling very sophisticated. The audience shouted, "Bravo! Bravo!" when he finished, just like they did at concerts in the movies.

But something was lacking. I thought I might find it in the theater. Once again I dressed up and ventured downtown on the subway by myself. I bought a ticket to a play. I knew it was a great play because it was by the two most famous playwrights—Rodgers and Hammerstein. It was called, *Me and Juliet*.

When I returned home, my mother asked me how I had fared.

"I don't know, ma . . . I didn't really like it . . . I don't think I like the theater . . . I don't see what's the big deal. It seems fake to me . . ."

But I did go again. I was desperate. Sometimes I struck it lucky, like the time I went to the ballet for the first time.

"You're going to the ballet?" my father said. "I never thought I'd see the day when a son of mine would go to the ballet." He wasn't trying to dissuade or shame me. He was just stating a fact. "You like that kind of stuff?"

"I don't know. That's what I'm trying to find out."

He shrugged his shoulders and went back to reading Jimmy Cannon in the *New York Post*.

I went to the New York City Ballet at City Center. Again by myself. I sat up in the sky. But this time I hit it right. *Medea*. Music by Bela Bartok. This time I applauded enthusiastically, out of genuine felt passion for what I had seen. It opened my eyes to new possibilities.

I struck it lucky again when Miss Morris, a local librarian, took a liking to me and recommended books she thought I might be interested in. One book she suggested was unusual, but in some way I intuitively understood it. I had always liked music and this book seemed like music to me. It was called *The Waves*. It was by an English woman named Virginia Woolf.

Then I joined a book club. After I bought the regular selection for several months, I received an unexpected book bonus: *Crime and Punishment* by Dostoevsky. For months I kept this book, unopened, on my shelf. I was afraid to look in it. Afraid to have, once and for all, my hopeless ignorance revealed. Dostoevsky, in our neighborhood, was a name that evoked suggestions of Einstein. Of the super-human mind. To attempt to read Dostoevsky hinted of the *hubris* one would display in bringing home the original version of *The Theory of Relativity*, and attempting to peruse it.

But one day curiosity got the better of me. I found I couldn't put the book down. I didn't comprehend all of what Dostoevsky was saying, but what I did get was absorbing and entrancing. I even gave a book report on it in our English class at Clinton and I became somewhat of a sensation since many of the other reports were on books like *The Dizzy Dean Story*.

One night at the YM-YWHA on the Grand Concourse, my friend Skinny Diamond dragged a girl named Donna Worshow up to me. Donna fancied herself an intellectual. She had been bragging about having read *A Stone For Danny Fisher* by Harold Robbins.

"Here, meet my friend Danny Schwartz," Skinny said. "You talk about reading. This guy is a brain."

"Oh, yeah," Donna said. She turned to me. "If you're so smart . . ."

"I didn't say I was so smart."

"Well your buddy here did. Look, if you're so smart, what was the last book you read?"

"Really . . . I mean, what's the difference?"

"Tell her," Skinny said.

"Yeah . . . I just read *A Stone For Danny Fisher.*"

"Oh, I read that. Did you like it?" I said.

"Tell her what *you* just read!" Skinny said.

"Yeah," Donna said.

"Well, I just read a book called *Crime and Punishment.* By Dostoevsky."

"What?" Donna said. *"What?"*

"*Crime and Punishment,*" I said, softly. "I didn't get it on purpose. I got it as a bonus book . . ."

"You couldn'a read that," Donna snapped. "You couldn'a read that." And she turned angrily and walked away without looking back.

Skinny laughed triumphantly. She'd been showing off at his expense. He was delighted with getting even with her. As for myself, I didn't know what to feel.

Chapter 30

We had many wonderful teachers at De Witt Clinton. Dedicated men and women who, often under difficult conditions, continued to struggle to get through to guys of different classes, races, and backgrounds, to struggle in a manner which I don't think it an exaggeration to call noble.

Some did this in the time-honored manner of good teachers everywhere. Others were more colorful.

My home room teacher was one of my favorites. Ed "Froggy" Lieberman was called Froggy because he was a small, balding, man, with a pot-belly, a round face and bulging eyeballs. He had a hoarse, raspy voice that sounded like he gargled each morning with hydrochloric acid.

Froggy taught physics. His classes, as well as my home room, were held in an atmosphere of amiable chaos. In home room, he didn't care whether you talked or not, or whether you stayed in your seat, as long as you didn't stray beyond certain tacitly defined norms which kept him out of trouble.

One of the guys in my home room was Philbert Pauley, the same Philbert who used to talk like Tonto and lead a gang of little kids to attack my brother and the other "accursed Nelsons" who lived on our street. I hadn't seen Philbert in several years. He was no longer the same young, blond, demented person he had once been. Now he had grown up. He was a very big, blond, demented person.

Half the guys in our home room were still in school only because

Froggy looked out for them. Froggy was loved by all the biggest, toughest guys in the school. If you took physics with Froggy, for example, all you had to do was come to class and you would get 90%. He graded on a scale of 0-10 and he added this to 90. You could even come fifteen minutes late to class every once in a while as long as you threw him some food for his lunch when you arrived. There was nothing secret about this. You just threw him, say, an apple or an ice cream pop as you walked in the door and then you could go to your seat and nothing would be said about it.

So Froggy was beloved. But, incredibly, on one morning, Philbert got into a scuffle with another guy in home room. When Froggy broke it up, Philbert began a venomous venting of his spleen on Froggy. Further enraged, Philbert charged down from his seat, attacked Froggy right in front of the room, and attempted to choke him. Well, this was *way* out of bounds. Everyone responded immediately. Five big mooks grabbed Philbert and pulled him off. As Froggy wandered around the front of the classroom, pale and choking, holding his throat and gagging, the mooks began to stomp Philbert on the floor. Then two black guys, Wilson Odom and "Pickles" O'Hare, took the cord that lifted the window shades through a pulley arrangement, and knotted it into a noose. The mooks brought Philbert over. They put the noose over his head, and they began to hang him, right there in the classroom. Fortunately, as Philbert began to choke, Froggy came back to his senses. Still holding his throat, he rasped, "Let him down, boys! Thanks, but LET HIM DOWN!"

The mooks released Philbert, throwing him on the floor where he lay holding *his* throat, gagging and disoriented.

"You better watch your ass," this big guy, Duke O'Mara said to Philbert when he had recovered sufficiently to return to his seat. Never again did he attempt to bother anyone in our home room. In fact, Philbert turned almost gentle after this.

One of the finest pleasures of being around Froggy was watching some of the toughest guys in the school respond to his live and let-live manner in an almost human fashion. Froggy did have one slightly weird stunt that was a trifle dangerous. On the last day of each month he ended class early. He picked up the metal wastebasket holding it so the open end faced the class. Then, for about a minute, you were allowed to throw coins at him, pennies, nickels, dimes, whatever. You tried to hit him with them as he ran back and forth in front of the classroom, attempting to dodge them and to protect his face with the wastebasket. He always got pelted pretty thoroughly, as coins came flying down from every direction and the class disintegrated into chaos, but after a short while everyone would run out of change and the game would stop, at which time Froggy would cease his hopping around and would gather up all the money which he kept as a small supplement to his income, along with the apples and the ice cream pops from the people who came late to class.

One guy in our homeroom class was a little, weak, loudmouth, with big ears and a big nose. He was named Stevie "Torpedo" Ratkin. Torpedo was from our neighborhood where he was famous for two things:

1. He was the only guy on the block who had ever punched out a girl.

2. When the girl, Dolores Del Garda, got up off the sidewalk, she had beaten the shit out of him.

Nonetheless, he still had a big mouth. His style was to find a powerful mook, like Duke O'Mara and follow him about, serving as a kind of court jester, while sharing, to some small extent, in Duke's power.

One day we were getting dressed in the locker room before gym class—Herbie, Louie, Torpedo, and myself. Herbie was raving. Someone had broken into his locker and stolen all his gym clothes. "I can understand the sneakers," Herbie said. "I can even understand taking my basketball trunks. But my *jock strap*? Why in the world would anyone want to steal my jock strap?"

While Herbie continued to fulminate, Torpedo slithered into the stairwell and pissed on the radiator. This was sanctioned by a long tradition at Clinton. If you felt lousy enough to want to stink up the place you could go piss on a radiator. The odor was so foul it made everyone else furious, and you were enabled to feel you had a certain potency in the world. That your presence made a difference.

Unfortunately though, Duke was going up the stairs. He cursed Torpedo vociferously for "stinkin' up my air." He was still surly when they got to the gym. Torpedo, to appease him, moved quickly to get him a basketball from the heavy oak chest in which they were kept. As Torpedo reached in for a ball, Duke closed the lid on his head.

It caught him at the ears and turned his head sideways. He was swearing bloody murder, but Duke wouldn't release his head until my Cousin Louie took pity on Torpedo and pried open the lid.

After this incident, Torpedo switched mooks and began to follow Louie around. Louie's main interest was betting on sports at this time. His second interest was movie magazines. His sister, Carol, bought them by the dozens, and he read each one. He had a crush on an actress named Terry Moore. When we kidded him, he wouldn't deny it. He would merely say, "I don't care what you guys think. I think she's adorable."

But his priority was gambling first, even before Terry Moore. He gambled every penny he earned with Abe the bookie. He never won. Then he got an idea: Why not take bets himself? He pooled his money with Torpedo and they began to run a baseball pool. You picked three players to get six hits on one day. They made a little money at this until one day at school a big group of guys led by Angie "The Hearse" Neopolitano placed extravagant bets on the same three players on the Boston Red Sox. Louie later found out that Boston had played a morning game that day. Angie had heard the highlights on his portable radio and he and his friends had bet after the fact.

Angie denied this. There was no way to prove it, so Louie paid off even though it wiped him out.

This depressed him, but he alleviated his sadness and embarrassment by working up a crazy mook Street Theater he played with Torpedo for a few weeks that amused everyone. Somehow he got his hands on a pair of crutches. Each night, when we all gathered to gossip and joke in front of the Noonan Plaza in the dark, he hid between two parked cars. When a car approached on Nelson Avenue, Louie suddenly sprang out into its path on his crutches. The driver shrieked to a stop. Louie threw his crutches up into the air, screamed, and fell flat on his back. He lay inert in the gutter, dead still. The driver, horrified, would burst out of his car in a panic to see what he had done, just as Torpedo appeared from across the street shouting, as outraged anguished bystander, "Oh, no, you've killed a cripple! You've run over a fucking cripple!"

No movement from Louie. Just when the driver was about to have a heart attack, the rest of us ran over from where we had been standing, and we shouted (outraged vehement crowd), "Oh, no, you killed a cripple!" Then Louie would suddenly leap up, grab his crutches, put them under his arm, and streak swiftly down the street, vanishing into the darkness like a deer, while we all cracked up at the sheepish dawning fury and relief on the driver's face.

Once again we young guys, car-less, powerless, and broke, had made a fool of an adult, a member of what seemed like another species, men who we fancied had control of their lives, and who we unconsciously held responsible for the sad state of ours.

Chapter *31*

When I visited my Aunt Rose after school, it was partly because it was quiet and calm at her place. No one was yelling at me or badgering me. She continued to live by herself in her parents' former apartment, and I came to look on her and her rooms as an island in a harried, speedy world. We would sit at the front window together, watching the street and most likely thinking of the past. Rose no longer spoke very often. She didn't generate the conversation, or reply with much more than a few words. She seemed to have been drained of everything, all hopes or anguishing disappointment or worries or fear. Perhaps the shock took them all away. I often wondered how it worked, and what it did to the memories, to the brain, to which part of the brain? How did they control it? How could it not help put out her spark and verve—how could it know just where *only* the fears were, without putting out also the hope which could fuel her to enter life? I only knew her spirit was still alive by the snatches of lovely old romantic songs she would quietly hum to herself as she shuffled around the darkness of her apartment rooms in battered slippers and an old flowered housedress. "That Old Feeling." "How Deep Is The Ocean?" "Again." She was a romanticist without an object of romance, a woman who had only been raised to charm without a place or person to love.

We sat by the window without speaking to one another. Some kind of silent communion took place. Perhaps it was that the quietness made out of her silences a time for introspection and puzzling. She was a mystery to me, a story gone wrong, and yet a kind woman—

151

the only one, in those years, around whom I could sometimes win a sense of clear, windless peace. Without speaking a word, we each were glad the other was there. We liked each other's *presence.* We looked at the same street with the stoplights she had used to teach me to spell. ("See the light, Danny. It's turned red. Spell *red,* Danny. OK, *good.* That's good. Now it's turned green. Spell *green.*"

I worried about my aunt, but her problems seemed way beyond my ken. Periodically the doctor would decide she needed more bone-jarring, memory-wiping shock treatments. But I was always able to locate a zone of ease and contentment during those times I sat with her, listening to her humming softly to herself, "It was just a masquerade ball, that's all that it was, but oh what it seemed to be . . ."

Rose seemed to me someone for whom life had simply not worked out, whether it was our family's or society's or The Bronx's fault. Had we not made room for her? Somehow created a climatic condition in which she could bloom? Later, when I read about Henry James' sister Alice, who was also sick all her life, his comment about Alice seemed to apply to Rose: "In our family group girls seem scarcely to have had a chance." He concluded about Alice, and I thought it also described Rose, ". . . her tragic health was, in a manner, the only solution for her of the practical problem of life."

I had always liked music. In my sophomore year, there occurred a great explosion in consciousness, an event that was to change the subsurface currents of my life and to provide me with a source of strength in many of the difficult days that followed. What I am referring to is the birth of the popularity of rhythm and blues music, the progenitor of rock and roll.

It began with Alan Freed on WINS. Having come to New York from Cleveland, he originated the "Moondog" show which became the center of interest, the guide and standard, virtually the religion, of hip teenagers from all over the New York area. De Witt Clinton, with so many students from Harlem, was one of the first territories to be enthralled, captivated, and, in some way, liberated, by this music which transformed every node and nexus of our lives.

For example, there were, at Clinton, seven large boys' bathrooms. Immediately, each was taken over by a vocal group, a quartet or quintet, who practiced their routines (sung harmony, synchronous hand jive, and simple, coordinated, dance movements) on Harlem street-corners at night, then performed them all day in the bathroom at school.

Suddenly school had become a theater, all day entertainment, pick your bathroom. Each group had its followers, and all were good. But it wasn't merely in the bathrooms. Rhythm and blues resounded everywhere, on subway platforms, in gym classes, and along the streets, and not from tinny loud portable radios but from live groups, right there. During lunch hours at Clinton we used to shoot foul shots outside for quarters with the guys from Harlem. Now, suddenly, we found ourselves shooting in rhythm to a line of black guys, standing on the base line, singing, "Hey, Senorita," by the Penguins (the flip side of "Earth Angel"). They would do a little African-inspired dance together, one foot behind the other, moving slowly back and forth along the edge of the court. They changed the song slightly so the background vocal, instead of going, "Ooo Ooo Ooo Ooo Ooo, Sweet Mama," went, "Ooo Ooo Ooo Ooo Ooo, eat mung," mung being a word for "ape shit," which was popular in the slang of the time.

Yes, everyone was dancing, swinging back and forth as they walked, and singing. You couldn't resist it. There was no getting away from it. It was home-made music, it was street corner music, it was black music, it was *our* music.

No more Debbie Reynolds and Perry Como and Tin Pan Alley for me. Now it was Frankie Lyman and the Teenagers from George Washington High, singing, "Why Do Fools Fall In Love?" It was, "This Is My Story," by Gene and Eunice. It was the Moonglows doing, "Sincerely," and, "We Go Together"; Laverne Baker singing, "Tweedle Dee Dee," and the "Late and Great" Johnny Ace singing, "Pledging My Love." It was the Clovers, "Devil or Angel?," the Heartbeats, "A Thousand Miles Away," the Nutmegs, "Story Untold," and the Harptones, "A Sunday Kind of Love."

It was the beginning of my connection with an underground of people in America who were reaching out for something electric and vibrant, something more than Vaughn Monroe and Kate Smith, something spontaneous which hinted of dangerous night streets, something that was lovely and throbbing and alive. It was five-foot-tall Clarence Tompkins from Harlem with his gold tooth shining brightly in the front of his mouth, walking beaming along the hallways of Clinton, in heaven as he sang, "They Often Call Me Speedo," with three six-foot string beans alongside him, doing a perfect hand jive and repeating the chorus behind him, "Mister Ear-l."

It transformed my radio into my closest friend and ally. No longer merely a consolation for my father's need to send me to bed before my friends, now the radio was a positive force. Now I *wanted* to be in my room by myself. Now I didn't mind being alone, because when I turned on my radio I wasn't lonely. I knew there were thousands of others out there listening just like me, and I felt that now I was tuning into what I had been looking for at last.

Although there were other disc jockeys, like Jocko from Harlem ("Eeee to the ock, I say here comes the Jock . . ."), it was Alan Freed who was at the center of this explosion for us. He gave us so much. I wish he were still here, on the Earth, where so many of us, once his children, could thank him.

Chapter 32

Going to a party in the East Bronx with four of the Philadelphians—Skinny Diamond, Herbie, Midge, and Louie, was a major event for me. I'd never been to a party in another neighborhood before. Skinny had dated the hostess and she was inviting four of her friends from Columbus High School to meet us. I hadn't gone out much with girls to this point. I spent most of my weekend evenings with Herbie, sitting on a stoop until two a.m., mulling over the possibilities of suicide and other heavy questions. Then we'd tell funny stories about the wacky people we knew, as if to prove and document the insanity of our world. My father didn't like this for some reason.

"What do you do out there, so late?"

"We just talk."

"You talk? Till two in the morning?"

"Yeah . . . It's interesting."

"How could you just talk?"

"I don't know . . . We talk."

"But what do you do out there?"

On the way to the party, Herbie kept telling us about how lucky the girls were that he was going to be in attendance and how he was "gonna get some" and so on. He sang old songs like, "Lulu's Back in Town," changing it to, "Mr. Herbie's Back in Town." He sang confidently about how Mr. Herbie regrets that there's not enough of him to go around.

We had dressed up in our best slacks and sport jackets. The girls wore new sweaters and skirts. We stood around in the living room of the girl's parents' apartment. No one knew what to do. We played, "Do you know so and so?" Then we put on cha-cha records and we danced to "Cherry Pink and Apple Blossom White," and "Papa Loves Mambo." Of course these records were "out" for those of us who were "cool," but we went along with it. Then we danced to slow music, all of us except Herbie, whose girl was almost six feet tall and had retreated to the kitchen. He had immediately insulted her inadvertently by saying she was "a lock" but he wouldn't want to take her into the pivot. Herbie, to save face, took over as disc jockey. Finally we all waited while Skinny and his girl necked for a while in the next room, and then we left. As we walked to the subway, Herbie went on talking: "Did you see the way the party changed when Mr. Herbie took over as D.J. and put on the slow music? Don't thank me, I do it for free . . ."

Not much had happened, but we loved the idea of it. We had actually been out on the town in New York with girls from another neighborhood until three a.m., or at least that was the way we felt when we finally got home, taking the subway back to Manhattan and then another subway up to the West Bronx. We walked in the moonlight talking about the girls in the quiet of the deserted night, feeling like "men about town."

As I entered my family's apartment, I felt a warm glow of satisfaction and growing maturity. A new world was opening up to me. Then there was this loud HUMP as my father jumped out of bed and my mother cried, "Sid, no!" My father appeared, running toward me, wearing only his old jockey shorts and an old, faded white undershirt. He began to hit me with a shoe he had in his hand, screaming, "It's three a.m. It's three a.m., you bastard," his face twisted and gnarled, his eyes glazed. There was no way I could reason with him. He was half-asleep and was running amok. I began to hop around the apartment as he chased me, his face in a frenzy of grimaces while he kept trying to beat me with his shoe, yelling, "It's three a.m."

I ran into my room and I slammed the door as hard as I could behind me. But the door wouldn't shut completely. Something was blocking it from closing. Something was stuck in the door. I looked up and saw, to my horror, that it was my father. I had caught him with the door. The door had closed across the front of his body, turning his head sideways, pinning him there by his chest and his left ear. His right hand was still free. He had the shoe in it, and as I held him there, pressing the door against him, he kept growling out of a gruesomely twisted red face while struggling to get at me with the shoe in his hand, like a crazed lobster.

It was a classic dilemma. I had to think quickly. Should I continue to squeeze my crazed father's head in the door and possibly injure him and maybe even make him *more* dangerous, or should I release him and suffer the consequences of my actions which now included not only coming home late, but catching my father's head in the door?

I held him for another second. My mother clutched at him from the other side, screaming, "Sid! Sid! Are you crazy?" Then I let go of the door and bent over, covering my head the way they had taught us to do in junior high school in case of an atomic bomb attack. I weathered the storm of blows until my mother got between us and finally brought him to his senses.

Now that I was taller than my father, this attack had proven, in actuality, to be more embarrassing than physically painful to me. Looking back on it, I imagine my father would not have noticed whether I was home or not unless my mother had remained awake fretting over me and he had gotten the idea that I was taking advantage of her in some way. She was the classic provocateur, goading him to fight her own battles in response to her anxiety. They were quite a Tin Pan Alley team in the old soft shoe of domestic abuse.

Chapter 33

It was about this time that Rosa Parks, a black woman, weary from having worked all day, refused to give up her seat and move to the back of the bus in Alabama. Thus began the Montgomery bus boycott and the modern American civil rights movement. Both Herbie and I were profoundly moved by this story, but it was Herbie who suggested we take some action. "This guy Martin Luther King," he said, "he's all right. He needs help. I think we should send him money."

Herbie and I began to skip going to the movies and to send the money saved to Martin Luther King. It wasn't much, but it meant a lot to us.

Besides Saturdays at Bernie's record store, Herbie was also working part-time in a drugstore. He didn't see my father much since my father was rarely at home, and when he was he would bury himself at the TV, watching sports and ignoring everybody. When they did talk, however, they would always argue. My father felt, I guess, that since Lenny was gone, he had to guide Herbie, while Herbie would use my father to try out his new ideas, advising my father to move to Greenwich Village where the real life was and so on.

But surprisingly, when my father wasn't around, Herbie would always defend him to me. "Your father loves you," he would say.

In the spring of 1955, my father made the final payments on the huge debt he had incurred almost ten years before when he had bought his half of the liquor store. He had staggered around under that backbreaking debt for as long as I could remember. Now he brought home the last notes and set them on fire in a pot on the kitchen stove. As they burned, flying pieces of the papers threatened to set the apartment on fire, so we had to rush to douse the flames and flush the remnants of the notes down the toilet.

My father had brought home a quart of Three Feathers. For the first time that I could remember, he got drunk. "No more goddamn debts!" he kept saying, while giggling in a strange way, until, unable to hold his liquor, he vomited into the toilet. He made hideous loud gargling noises and finally passed out on the tiled bathroom floor.

Two months later, he had borrowed tens of thousands of dollars and had gone even more deeply into debt, in order to buy out his partner and become sole owner of his store. Since he would have to run the store now without his partner, with just Armando his clerk, this meant he would have to work even longer hours than he had in the past.

He liked his status as sole owner of the store. He went along with my mother's suggestion that they buy a new car more fitting for a man of his position. They bought a huge white Oldsmobile 98. When he taught my mother to drive, she swung too wide turning into narrow Shakespeare Avenue and ran into a parked car. Flustered, she stepped on the gas rather than the brakes, further driving that parked car into the two cars in front of it, to the delight and hilarity of dozens of spectators. My father suddenly regretted all those horses under the hood. But when he bought it, he was happy as the birds we sometimes saw on TV.

Even though my father's outward appearance was classier, his character didn't change overnight. A bit later, we got a call from Hector, a policeman at the liquor store.

"Mrs. Schwartz, you gotta talk to you husband. It ain't right, Mrs. Schwartz."

"What's wrong?"

"It's Sid, Mrs. Schwartz. He attack a junkie here in the street. The junkie, Luis, was kidding him. Said, 'I hear you bought out you son at the liquor store.' He mean Sid's partner. So Sid say, 'You think I'm old? I show you who's old,' and he jump Luis the junkie, and when I come they rolling in the gutter."

"Oh, no."

"He OK, Mrs. Schwartz. And I no arrest him. But it don't look right, Mrs. Schwartz. He a respected citizen in the neighborhood here. It don't look right for him to attack no junkie in the gutter."

My mother took a cab to the store and berated my father for this, but Luis the junkie had not been completely wrong in his perception of my father. There was no denying it, my father was aging quickly. How many times had my mother herself related to me with delight that someone had come to the door and asked to speak to her father, meaning Sid?

In May of 1955, I became batboy for the Cincinnati Reds at the Polo Grounds. I got the job for a day—a doubleheader on a Sunday— through my friend Midge Waxenthal, the Giants' batboy. Midge had been the batboy for the Giants during their miracle world championship year of 1954 and it was during that season that my association with the Giants had begun. Midge and I journeyed to the Polo Grounds after school to sign baseballs in the clubhouse for the veterans in hospitals. We each practiced imitating the players' signatures and we specialized in half the team apiece.

In a way, I guess you could say this was my first experience in writing fiction. I took on the identity of other characters, imitating them, and writing words for them. People believed it was true, and it made these people happy. No one was hurt by it.

On the day of the game, I went to the park early and put on my Cincinnati uniform, number 99. I went out onto the field for the Giants' batting practice. Not sure where to go, I wandered into the outfield.

When I reached my position in center field, a muscular man, about my height, perhaps a little shorter, trotted my way and stopped a few feet to my right. When I looked at his face, I saw he was Willie Mays.

Just then, the batter hit a fly ball toward deep right-center field. I took off after it. Willie Mays took off after it, too, but I was closer. Before I realized what I was doing, I shouted, "I got it, Willie!" He pulled up and stood back as I caught the ball and threw it into the infield. He went back to his position.

And suddenly, it occurred to me, what I had done. I, Danny

Schwartz of Nelson Avenue, had waved off Willie Mays, arguably the best all-around baseball player that has ever lived, and I had caught a ball in his territory, center field at the Polo Grounds, a huge pasture which he *owned,* which, in its immensity, seemed almost to have been built just for him to have the space to show off his amazing talents in front of millions of people. I had shouted, "I got it, Willie," and I had caught the ball just like that.

I didn't know what to make of it. On the one hand, I feared that I was in the wrong place, taking Willie's space; on the other hand, there was Willie, back at his position over to my right, not complaining, acting like I had done just what I should have by calling for a ball that was mine.

And I did catch it. And as I stood there, I began to feel very good about what had happened. Nothing else that happened that day or for years afterward quite touched that catch.

That summer, just before my senior year, I finally got to go to camp. Camp Merryglade, in the Catskills near Monticello, was Skinny Diamond's camp. Although he had no father, Skinny had somehow managed to go there for years. I was sixteen years old and was to be a counselor-in-training. This meant that I would only have to work half-time and that my father would only have to pay half the standard fee. In a way, this wasn't such a bad deal, since I was given room and board for the whole summer and both my father and I knew that I would get paid for being a counselor there after I graduated from high school.

I lived in a little room behind the stage in the recreation hall. I shared the room with a guy named Henry Taub, the music counselor. He went to Music and Art High School in the City. He loved classical music, especially Bach, and he lamented the fact that the favorite song of 90% of the people in the camp was, "This Is My Beloved." When I talked to him about the Penguins and the Cadillacs, he used to say to me, "You like Boogie-Woogie. I like Bachy-Wachy."

He wanted to be a concert pianist when he grew up, to play in Carnegie Hall and tour the world. When he left camp at the end of the summer, he stole my suitcase.

There was one girl at camp, Sue Ellen Broder, who was rumored to be a "nympho," but I suspect no one at the camp had much experience at "going all the way" with any girl, much less a nympho. There was a great deal of sex at the camp, but little going all the way. It usually wound up with the guy coming in his pants on top of the girl out on the softball field.

In some ways, this was better than going all the way. If you went all the way, there was no evidence of it, but if you came in your pants, then later, at curfew, when all the boy counselors checked in together, you could join the ranks of the successful by virtue of being one of the group who had big wet stains on their tan chinos, about which everyone would kid you good-naturedly in a manner which was clearly a backhanded compliment.

Herbie and Louie were in the Catskills that summer, too. They visited Skinny and me at Camp Merryglades on visiting days. Louie had graduated from Clinton and was working feverishly at Tamarind Lodge to pay back gambling debts. He planned to get a regular job in the fall, but he owed so much money to people from whom he had borrowed to pay Abe the bookie, that he had decided to spend one last summer in the Catskills where he could make more money. He had three jobs. He was a waiter, a tough enough job under any circumstances, up at six in the morning, working on and off until eight in the evening. Besides this, he also shagged golf balls on the driving range during the afternoon, and then, at night, from eight to midnight, he worked in the snack bar. It was a schedule only a mook could handle. Just when all the other waiters would be catching up on their sleep for an hour or two, Louie would be going to his second or third job. When he collected balls on the driving range, he wore a wire-mesh "space suit" to protect him, but it backfired in a way since everyone used him as a target for their drives. Finally, the manager of the range took advantage of this by offering a five dollar prize for anyone who could hit him.

One reason Louie was in the country was that he felt that if he was away from the city and always working he would have less opportunities to bet. He had become addicted to betting in a bad way, one of those people who are always going double or nothing to try to catch up and thus fall further behind.

Herbie, at seventeen, had just finished his first year at Hunter College. He hadn't done well. He had barely passed. Instead of

162

studying, he stayed up all night listening to Jean Shepherd on the radio. He spent his days moping around his house with the existentialists and fried bananas. At the beginning of the summer he decided to drop out of school. He got himself a full-time job loading crates onto trucks at a factory in the East Bronx. On weekends he came to Tamarind Lodge where he stayed for free with the assistance of Louie. He would eat at one of the tables Louie served and he would sleep in Louie's bed in the waiters' quarters when Louie wasn't there, which was most of the time. The funny side of this was that by the end of the summer Herbie had been at Tamarind for so many weekends, most of the staff thought he was a regular guest and they all treated him very well. This proved to be his undoing, as he convinced *himself,* apparently, that he was a regular guest. On Labor Day weekend, he complained about the quality of the food to the management. He was passed up the hierarchy until finally someone had the sense to say, "Who the hell *is* this guy, anyhow?" They called in the sheriff, who put Herbie in the slammer.

The hotel owners settled the issue without pressing charges when Louie agreed to pay the cost of all Herbie's weekends out of his own salary. Herbie agreed to pay Louie back out of his meager salary as a crate loader. Louie was fired, but it didn't really matter. He was about to begin to fund his gambling fever with funds earned from working in the billing department of a Manhattan dressmaking firm.

Chapter *34*

At the end of summer, my Cousin Herbie surprised us by joining the Marines.

"Gee," I said, "the Marines . . ."

"Someone's got to defend this country," he said, quietly. "It's a tough job, but someone's gotta do it."

He had two months before he reported for basic training. We talked a lot. One night when he was over at my house, we drifted into the living room where my mother was watching the end of the Miss America contest. As the contest concluded with the new Miss America walking down the aisle to the cheers of the multitudes while Bert Parks sang, "Here she comes, Miss America . . . ," my mother stood up and began to walk slowly around the living room, regal in her bearing, an imaginary bouquet of flowers held against her body by her left arm, waving to thousands of imaginary people with her right, smiling, beaming with pleasure. I was surprised to see real tears in her eyes.

She continued her little parade to the music until she was interrupted by a kind of loud but stifled gargling in the street. "Oh my God," she said. "It's your father." She rushed to the window. We stood up to follow but she turned to us and shouted, "Help him, boys. Help him. They're killing him."

We ran down the stairs, three at a time, across the street to where a man was choking my father through the window of my father's car which was nose-first, half-way into a parking space. My father and the man were both red-faced and growling, and my father was struggling to get at the man's throat.

The choker wasn't that big a man. Herbie and I had no trouble pulling him off. The chokee just sat there in his car, trying to catch his breath, rubbing his throat with both his hands. The choker's brother-in-law came along in a huge Buick. After some face-saving shouting by both parties to the fight, the choker got into the Buick and they drove off.

What had happened became clear when my father recovered sufficiently to explain. My father, as befitted his lifestyle, always refused to pay the monthly fee to park in the lot on the next block. He often worked late, sometimes until midnight, so it usually took him close to an hour to find a parking space. There were slightly more cars than parking spaces in The Bronx, and it was amazing to me that sometimes he didn't have to drive around all night without finding one. But he would ultimately locate one and would then walk the six or eight blocks home. If we were awake when he arrived, we could recognize his cough as he approached. It was always quiet at night, and as he smoked more than two packs of cigarettes a day, we could hear him gagging as he came up the street.

On this particular evening he had left the store early, leaving Armando to close up. He cruised around for almost an hour when he spied a parking place. A large spot, a beautiful spot, right across the street from our house. There was only one problem. There was a man standing in it.

"Excuse me, buddy. I'm gonna park here."

"No," the guy said, shaking his head. "No good."

"No good? Whaddya mean, no good?"

"I'm saving it for my brother-in-law."

"You're *what*?"

"My brother-in-law. He went to get his car. He's parked over by a pump on Shakespeare Avenue."

"Whaddya talking about, your brother-in-law? Move outa there, buddy. First come, first serve."

The man wouldn't move, and my father was getting steamed. He could see the spot, right there. *His* spot. But the man standing in it was *trying to take advantage of his good nature.*

So he backed up slightly, pointed his Oldsmobile at the man, and said out the window in a quiet but minatory tone, "Look buddy, I'm gonna park here. This is my spot. If you're still standing there, I'll run you down."

"Up yours!" the guy said. My father slammed on the gas, the big car lurched forward. The man barely leaped out of the way into the gutter, rolled over, jumped up, reached through the window into the car, and began to choke my father.

You know the rest. After my father went to bed, Herbie and I continued to talk. He kept going on and on about the Marines, but my mind was still on my father, who had nearly run a man down because of his frustration over not finding a parking spot. I couldn't say it to Herbie, but the Marines just seemed a bigger version of my father, organized into official venom but with the same crazy half-cocked ignorance and "might is right" attitudes.

Herbie was caught up in the romance of the Marines from his movies and novels. He was as much in dreamland as Rose, but certified healthy and ready to kill. Such was the easy life of the street tough—we just glided into the services as though they were one more neighborhood to take on.

Herbie worshipped Private Robert E. Lee Prewitt, the bugler and boxer in *From Here To Eternity*. Prewitt was Regular Army, not Marines, but Herbie loved Prewitt. He also loved Montgomery Clift who played Prewitt in the movie. Herbie saw the movie whenever he could and he read the book again and again. He had even taken to playing an imaginary bugle when he had nothing to do. He would shuffle around, shadow boxing while reciting Prewitt's lines from the movie, probably imagining he *was* Montgomery Clift as Prewitt.

I couldn't help but feel a certain awe at the rash boldness which Herbie had shown in leaping so precipitously into adulthood, but my overriding feeling was deep sorrow. Where would Herbie find room for his eccentric brilliance, his coruscating sarcasm, and his occasional winsome charm in the Marines?

It was Herbie's charm that my mind lingered on that night. I thought of the time he had led me to Basin Street, the large Times Square night club, to see Duke Ellington's band. Although Herbie read *Downbeat* regularly, we had never seen live jazz before. We lied about our age and stood with the hipsters at the bar. When a well-dressed, jovial, somewhat rotund black man approached, Herbie looked up and said, "What do you say, Bill?"

The man broke into an amused, slightly ironic, big laugh and happily patted Herbie on the shoulder as he passed.

"Who was *that*?" I said, amazed.

"Count Basie," Herbie said, nonchalantly.

"*Count Basie*? But you called him Bill."

"His real name's not *Count*!" And then Herbie added, as if it were painfully obvious, "All of his friends call him Bill, Danny."

I made no attempt to deflate Herbie's dreams, but when he proudly told Louie he had joined the Marines, Louie replied, matter of factly, "Whaddya, nuts?"

Chapter *35*

Early in November of that year, an event occurred in our neighborhood which affected me deeply. I still remember that it happened on a Wednesday night because it was the day after the election.

It was the trial of Pop Goldman in the gym at P.S.11. Pop's problem had begun in September. The Philadelphians were beginning to drift apart. The older guys like my cousins were already out of school, working or going into the service. The rest of us, like Midge, Skinny, Huge Marvin, and myself were seniors in high school. The end of our affiliation as the Philadelphians was clearly in sight.

This threatened to leave an empty place in Pop's life. He lived by himself in the East Bronx, and we boys in Highbridge had constituted a kind of surrogate family for him. He never talked about any acquaintances in the East Bronx and I doubt that he had many. It seemed he was always in our neighborhood. Everyone knew him. He had been coming to Highbridge for years, first with the original Philadelphians, and then with us. With him as our leader we had stuck together for six years, saving our money, buying jackets and uniforms, meeting regularly, learning the rules of "parliamentary procedure," and playing road games which he arranged for us in places like Bayonne and Hoboken, New Jersey. And always, after a game on the road, he would take us out and buy each of us an ice cream or a piece of pie. It wasn't that we couldn't afford to buy them ourselves. It was just his way of saying thanks to us for what we gave him.

In September he formed a new team. The kids were eleven and twelve years old. Just about the age we were when we had first gotten together. He called them the Philadelphians, too.

A few weeks later rumors of trouble began to circulate through the neighborhood. The chief source was a man named Morris Plankton, a little guy with a huge Adam's apple and a big mouth who worked as a clerk for the Internal Revenue Service. His son was on Pop's new team. Morris claimed that Pop had stared at his son for too long in the shower after a game. Morris grilled the other boys and some of them admitted to feeling the same way. As this story spread throughout the neighborhood, feelings ran high and people talked of little else.

The fathers of the other boys also became enraged and they joined with Morris to do something about it. Perversity in Greenwich Village was one thing, but this was The Bronx! And it was *their sons.* So they confronted Pop. They told him what they were accusing him of. They offered to try him themselves, in a "kangaroo court," rather than turn him over to the police.

Pop denied everything, but rather than face the police, he submitted to their trial. Morris Plankton would be the judge. Philly Samuels, who owned a fish store over on Brook Avenue in the East Bronx, would be the attorney for the defense. Sol Nissoff, who worked in a United Cigar Store over in Manhattan, would be the attorney for the prosecution.

The trial was a farce. There was really no need for it. Pop was already a broken man when he arrived. There was no reason to proceed. But, of course, they did.

They had arranged the gym to look like a courtroom on TV, setting up chairs and benches and a table for Morris the judge. Morris had a heavy wooden mallet from Philly's fish store to use to keep order. They selected a jury of "Pop's peers." The jury was all male. There were no women present in the gym.

They paraded the kids up as witnesses for the prosecution. The kids, shyly, and under prodding, said tentatively, "I think so," and, "I guess so." Then they paraded adults up to give circumstantial evidence. Wasn't Philadelphia the city of brotherly love? Did Pop have a family of his own? Had anyone ever seen him out on a date? Was there even one man in the room who would have worried had Pop visited his house and found his wife home alone?

The attorney for the defense, Philly Samuels, began by stating, "I want you all to know that I don't condone what this guy did one bit. Not for one minute. But he deserves a fair trial in accord with the rules of our land. So I'm gonna try to defend him."

He called to the stand those of us who were willing to speak in Pop's behalf. Most of the Philadelphians could only say, "I don't know. He never bothered me." Pop himself didn't testify. He said he was "too choked up." He merely sat there silently, looking small and broken and alone, with tears in his once-twinkling blue eyes.

Unfortunately, my Cousin Herbie couldn't testify because he was in boot camp on Parris Island. I would have loved to have heard what he would have said. They saved me for last in his place since they thought I would be the most articulate, but I lost my composure as soon as I took the stand and looked at Pop, so pitiable there, sitting by himself. I began screaming at them, "What are you doing? Do you know what you're doing? What are you *doing* to this man?" Morris banged his fish hammer on the table and ruled me out of order. I shouted, "Fuck you, Morris. *You're* the one who's out of order," and I walked off the stand.

The jury deliberated in the locker room behind the gym for ten minutes. They found Pop guilty. Morris delivered a pompous speech thanking them and thanking Philly Samuels for helping to give Pop a fair trial in the American tradition. Then he said, "Will the defendant please rise for sentencing?"

Pop stood up, looking down at his feet and not saying a word.

"This is a terrible thing you've done," Morris said. "A terrible thing. This is a sad day for me, but this must not go unpunished. These boys are the future of our neighborhood. When you violate their trust, you not only violate them, you violate their parents and this great country of ours. Nevertheless, the court must, in all fairness, take into consideration your years of service to the people of this neighborhood. Therefore, in the interests of mercy as well as justice, we will not turn you over to the cops. The court hereby sees fit to banish you from the neighborhood for life. If you are ever seen again in Highbridge, you will be turned over to the cops. But for now, it is the court's belief that you should be made a free man, but I for one hope I never set eyes on you or your kind again."

170

Pop continued to look down at his feet as he said, in a soft voice, "Thank you, your honor."

I don't know what happened to me. I guess it was hearing that, "Thank you, your honor," that did it. I heard myself scream, "Morris, you fucker!" and I rushed at him. He hopped off his chair and put the table between us as Skinny and Marv and a couple of the men ran over and grabbed me. I fought, without success, to pull my arms free. As Morris backed off with fear in his eyes, I screamed at everyone, "You fuckers! How could you do this? He bought us pies, you bastards!" I continued to struggle to pull free, but they held me. "He kept us together, you bastards," I shouted. "He was like a father to us. He took us to Bayonne, New Jersey, you bastards. He was like a father to us."

"Hey, take it easy, Danny," Skinny said, holding me back, "Take it easy."

"You take it easy," I screamed at him. Crying now with rage, I pulled my arms loose, throwing Skinny off me, but instead of charging Morris again, I just turned around and walked out the door.

I don't know how far I walked. I was crying and angry and not paying attention to where I was going. I had to be pretty much out of my mind, because before I knew it I was at Johnny Murphy's candy store at the top of the hill on 170th Street. I must have been wandering about for a long time because it suddenly seemed much later than I expected. If I had been in my right mind, I never would have gone that way. It was the hangout of the Ikes. Their territory. They lingered outside the store every night, and since they knew it was not on my way to anywhere, since I had to go out of my way to get there, my appearance there, late at night, by myself, was clearly a challenge to their power and an affront to their masculinity.

I didn't notice Little Jimmy Carruthers until I bumped into him. "Hey, beating up on a little guy," Hammerhead Morgan said, with a hideous smile on his face. Hammerhead had become their leader. He had changed little over the years. Even among morons he stood out. He still looked like a vicious sicko bred in the swamp of night. "And look at this. He's crying," Hammerhead said, mockingly. "This poor son of a bitch is crying, he's so frightened." They all laughed at me. "You ain't got nothing to cry about . . . yet." They laughed. "We just don't like you picking on Little Jimmy here."

They gathered around me in a square. There were four of them, plus Little Jimmy who was in the center with me. Little Jimmy wasn't all that little. He was about five foot six, well-built. He was circling me, gloating like a depraved elf.

The two Ikes behind me pushed me into him. I lost my balance and he hit me a shot in the chest. I fell backwards into the two guys who had pushed me. They shoved me forward again and he hit me again, but as I flew back and forth, something snapped in me, some location on the grid of rationality was lost, and on hot impulse I punched out, I punched out with all the fury that had been tightening inside of me for years. As I was thrust toward Jimmy, flying forward from another hard shove by his friends, I threw a straight hard right that slammed into him. Maybe I had bashed in his face.

He fell back screaming, "My nose! He broke my fuckin' nose." Hammerhead ran over to him. The other three guys grabbed me. Two of them put me against the wall, holding my arms and shoulders right next to the plate-glass window of Johnny Murphy's store, while the third began to punch me in the belly, knocking the wind out of me.

"Wait, Tommy, save him for little Jimmy," the guy on my right said.

"Yeah, let Jimmy smash the fucker."

As I regained my breath, I looked up and I saw the huge white Oldsmobile at the stoplight on the corner, about to come down the street and pass in front of us. It was my father. Driving around the quiet neighborhood, looking for a parking space. The whole possible scenario laid itself out before my eyes. After all those years of beating me and of random attacks on strangers, my father's craziness was finally going to be put to use. My father would see me. He would stop the car, fling open the door and come rushing at the Ikes with such a strange, wild, look on his face, charging at them with such mad abandon that their blood would freeze. He would start pulling the bastards off me, and I would join with him. Hammerhead and Little Jimmy would attack us, but I would throw Little Jimmy through the plate-glass window, and my father and I would look at each other for one swift second. In that look would be all the love and loyalty to each other that a lifetime together had built up, and we would go at the Ikes together, me and my Pop. We would wipe out the fuckers.

"Come on, Jimmy, take care of this fucker," the goon on my left said to Little Jimmy who was still touching his face where I had hit him.

My father started up his car on my right. He drove along the street, moving slowly past me from my right to my left. I couldn't call to him. I was too old for that. I couldn't say, "Pop, help me. Pop, I need help," because it wouldn't have been worth it. There was no dignity to it. Even though I was outnumbered, I couldn't call for my father. It was something a kid would do. He had to see me on his own and rush the fuckers who were holding me against the wall. As he passed, I could see his face. He was looking straight ahead. And I knew what was on his mind: "If I pay the $3500 to Simkus, and then I take a second mortgage for $8000 at 4%, and then I pay the note I owe Bronx County Trust for $500, and then I pay my brother Sol $600, I'll still owe Weintraub $1000, but I can take a Christmas bonus from the store for $250 and so if I give Ceil $65 for food next week, and I make $2000 gross on the store next week . . ."

He passed me right by. He never once looked in my direction. I saw the broad back of his big car as the red taillights moved smoothly off and he drove out of sight. Again something in me snapped. I wrenched away from the two guys who were holding me, and I hit the third moron a glancing right to the ear. He swung back at me as the other two guys started grabbing for me, and then the four of us sprung into a jumbled ruckus. Amazingly, I held my own for a while, throwing lefts and rights wildly, but then they began to pummel me. Then Johnny Murphy and a friend of his and his two teenage sons ran out of the store. Johnny lived on our block. He recognized me, and he and his sons worked to pull the Ikes off of me. The Ikes got in a few more blows and a couple kicks, but they respected Johnny and they wouldn't mess with him. People began to turn on their lights and open their windows, shouting, "What's goin' on? I'm tryin' to sleep, you sons of bitches," and suddenly the street was becoming illumined from all the lit windows. More people were shouting, and even the Ikes could see the moment was over. It was time to wrap up this sorry episode before the cops came and took us all in.

As I walked home, I was beginning to feel the soreness in the parts of my body which they had punched and kicked. My right fist ached from where I had hit Jimmy Carruthers. Nonetheless, I felt good in a way, glad that I had stood up for myself, and that Johnny Murphy and his boys had come out to help me. And I knew my father would have helped me, too. I *knew* it. He would have come rushing over, and we would have stood there together and smashed the shit out of the Ikes, he and I, together. I knew he would have helped me. If only he had seen me.

Chapter **36**

When I got home, my mother was still awake, waiting up to make my father his late-night dinner of eggs and onions. She screamed bloody murder when she saw me. I looked in the mirror and saw that I had streaks of blood finger-painted across my face. But in spite of her hysteria, I felt all right. I felt calm, somehow. Quietly satisfied, and spent. When my father walked in, she shouted at him, "Look at this boy! Look at what they did to him! He's a brilliant boy. He doesn't need this. We gotta get him out of here. Do you hear me? We gotta get him out of here!"

The following Sunday, my mother gave my brother money to go to the movies, and we had a family meeting, she and I and my father. We sat down at the kitchen table. She had put out an apple cake, a cheese cake, and a Hostess pound cake. No one was going to starve even if this took all afternoon. But it didn't take more than a few minutes, actually.

"Your mother says you want to go to an out-of-town college," my father said.

"Yeah . . . I'd like to, but it's expensive."

My mother gave my father a sharp glance.

"Don't worry about expense," my father said. "I'll worry about expense."

"He's not staying around here," my mother said. "And that's that. I want Danny out of this neighborhood."

"All right. All right, already," my father said, in an annoyed tone.

"Whaddya wanna be, Danny? I mean when you grow up."

"I don't know, Pop."

"Well, look . . . You gotta wanna be something. I mean, I'm not sending you off to college, and spending thousands of dollars, unless you wanna be something. I'm not gonna slave away here and go into debt so you can read poems for four years."

"I don't know, Pop."

"You wanna be a doctor?"

"No . . . I don't."

"A lawyer?"

"No, Pop."

"Well, what then? Whaddya wanna be?"

"What else is there?"

"I don't know," my father said, turning to my mother. "What else could he be?"

My mother thought for a few seconds. "An accountant? Maybe he could be an accountant."

"No," I said. "I don't like it."

"Well, what can we do?" my father said. "If he's gonna go to college, he's gotta be something. I can't send him to hang around and do nothing. I'd be the laughingstock of the neighborhood. Everybody would say to me, 'You're wasting thousands of dollars while that bum of a son of yours is hanging around with rich kids.' I'd never live it down."

"How about an engineer?" I said.

"An engineer?" my father said, with interest. "An engineer . . . That sounds good. Tell me Danny, what does an engineer do?"

"I don't really know, Pop. I think it has something to do with math and science."

"Math and science!" my mother said, seeing her opportunity. "He's first in chemistry and physics in his whole school. He's gonna win the medals at graduation. And he's second in math. It's perfect for him, Sid. It's perfect."

"Yeah, Dad . . . It's perfect for me . . . It has to do with math and science, I think . . ."

My father's face began to brighten. "An engineer," he said, savoring the words, seeming to taste them as they rolled out over his tongue. "An engineer . . . My son . . . An engineer . . . " He turned to my mother, a look of glee suffusing his face. "They'll all say I'm crazy. They'll say I'm nuts." He was getting happier and happier. "I'll have to borrow thousands of dollars . . . They'll all say I'm out of my mind. My sister Fanny . . . Hilda . . . My brother Sol . . . Your brother Bernie." He was practically glowing with delight. "I'll have to slave at the store. I'll have to do without. I'll have to go into debt and struggle. But someday, someday in the future, he's gonna pull up at our house here in the street, and he's gonna be in a new Pontiac convertible, and his wife is gonna be at his side and his kids in the back, and the whole neighborhood's gonna be watching outa their windows, and he's gonna come to visit me, an engineer, and after he goes, I'm gonna go outside, and I'm gonna say to them all, 'You said I was crazy. You said I was nuts to send him to an out-of-town college. Well, now he's an engineer. So who's crazy now?' I'll say to them. 'My son is an engineer. Now who's crazy, smart guys? Now who has the last laugh?' "

He turned to me, and he said, smiling, "Find a good school. Make out the application. You're going to be an engineer."

Chapter *37*

I was often lonely during my senior year in high school. Herbie was gone. I had no one to talk seriously with. Louie was working and, although I sometimes saw him at night, and still played basketball with him once in a while, he often worked overtime to pay off his gambling debts. He continued to bet heavily; he always lost. He kept trying to make "one big killing," but he never did, and he fell further and further behind. It wasn't in his nature to borrow money from people easily, and this began to feed on his once happy and basically good-natured temperament.

There were a couple strange fads in the neighborhood that were interesting for a while. One was throwing eggs. For a month, no one went out in the street without carrying a dozen eggs. Eggs were flying all over in every direction. In a way, it actually reduced the violence for a time. Whenever anyone was insulted, he would run into a grocery store, buy a dozen eggs, and let the other guy have it. The whole neighborhood began to resemble a giant omelette, with egg whites and yokes flying in every direction but even though eggs were cheap, they weren't free, so eventually this fad petered out.

Another fad was playing tackle football without helmets or equipment on the cobblestones of 170th Street. This got started as a joke one day, but it proved to be less dangerous than we had imagined, as long as you were careful not to smash a guy's head against the stones when you tackled him. The game stopped when Sonny Silverman, always known for his outrageously inspired play in all sports, ran a slant off tackle for a score, putting his head down and bucking toward the right through the line, ready to carry people with him into the end zone. Not one person got a hand on him, but he slanted a bit too far to the right, and he ran full speed, headfirst into a cast-iron lamp post. He had to be rushed to Morrisania Hospital to get his head sewn back together.

After his initial enthusiasm, my father began to resent my going to college. He didn't see me very often, since he was at his store most of the time, but when he did see me he would give me needless chores to do and he would call me, "Boula-Boula."

"Hey, Boula-Boula, just because you're gonna be a college man don't mean you can't straighten up your room."

"I did straighten it up. Yesterday."

"Straighten it up again, Boula-Boula."

I wasn't going to Yale, but to him that's what all colleges were: "Boula-Boula" for four years and then a free ride for the rest of your life.

But if he bothered me too much, I could always retreat to my room and read the works of my big brothers and sisters, the American novelists. Or listen to rhythm and blues, or to Symphony Sid, playing my new love, modern American jazz, all night on the radio. I slid into the warm reassuring tones of Charlie Parker, Miles Davis, Chet Baker and company, leaving the rasping cuts of my father outside to find some other target.

In the spring, as I prepared to leave high school and The Bronx to begin another phase of my life, my Aunt Rose was admitted to Montefiore Hospital. During the previous year she had begun to lose control of her body. They diagnosed her condition as multiple sclerosis. The family had hired the same live-in nurse to take care of her that they had hired when my grandmother had fallen apart.

Rose had little resistance. She had not exercised for years, unless you could call twitching on the table when they jammed electricity into your brain "exercise." She deteriorated quickly. In the hospital she wanted no visitors, and the family was not anxious for anyone but the closest relatives to see her "until she's well again." In June, however, the family decided to have a gathering at her bedside to show

179

her how much the family cared. No "kids" were to come except myself, because she had asked to see me.

We went to the hospital together, on a Sunday afternoon, in a line of cars. We were late in leaving because my father was balancing his checkbook for one of the buildings and he was short $100 somewhere. He couldn't locate it, and it was driving him nuts. Finally, my mother suggested he take the checkbook along, which he did. Then there was another delay because my Uncle Bernie was drunk, and my Aunt Evelyn from Brooklyn didn't want to drive with him, so she and my Uncle Sol had to be switched to another car.

But we finally made it to the hospital. Everyone was there. My Uncle Bernie, who kidded with the nurse, my Aunt Bessie, my Cousin Bert who worked at Bernie's store and his wife Sarah, Sol and Evelyn ("Don't put your ass in my face") who had come all the way from Brooklyn to our house on the subway, my Aunt Fanny, my Uncle Albee, the taxi driver, and his wife Hilda, my father's sister who always beat up her son. Even our Cousin Dora from Brooklyn, the 300-pound woman who had gotten drunk and stuck on the stairs at my *bar mitzvah*. She was slightly drunk again. She giggled and laughed loudly as my Uncle Bernie kept trying playfully to feel her up as a way of avoiding looking at my Aunt Rose. And over in the corner, at a little white table they had brought in, trying to locate the hundred dollars in the checkbook with a scowl on his face, sat my father.

My Aunt Rose lay like a tiny used up child in her hospital bed. She looked so small, I couldn't believe it. She was limp, lying immobile, under the covers. She looked like a stuffed doll that had leaked out its insides and had been thrown away. She looked like she had shrunk.

Her face was frightened and pale. Gray and helpless and dolorous. She was no longer living in the same world as the rest of us.

"Go stand there near her, so she can see you," my mother said.

I complied, moving over next to her, near the head of the bed.

"You see," my mother said, "she's getting better." Then to my aunt, lying there so small and terrified, "You'll be out of here in no time. Doesn't she look good?" my mother said to my aunts. "She'll be back on her feet before we know it."

"She sure does," my Aunt Evelyn said. "There ain't nothin' wrong with her that a little rest won't cure."

"There ain't nothing wrong with her that a little of *this* won't cure," my Uncle Bernie said, making an Italian "fuck you" sign with his arms. My drunken Cousin Dora laughed loudly and even Bernie's wife Bessie and my Aunt Fanny couldn't resist a smile. My Aunt Rose still didn't respond.

"I'll tell you one thing," my father said, looking up, ignoring the ashes from his cigarette falling into his lap, "she's getting the best medical care money can buy."

"But it's worth every cent," my mother said. "Look at her. She always was the beauty of the family and now you can see it again. She's getting more beautiful than ever. She'll be out of here and she'll be married and have kids of her own some day, you watch and see."

"She sure will," my childless Aunt Evelyn said.

"I think we should get a young doctor in here to give her some real treatment at night," my Uncle Bernie said. "Then she'll be better in a couple days." Everyone laughed except Aunt Rose, myself, and my father, who was adding up a column of figures.

And then my Aunt Rose moved. This little bundle of life, almost hidden under the covers, helplessly watching it all, moved her right arm toward me. I took her hand in mine. She looked over at me and she smiled. Yes, she smiled. At me. And then she spoke, in a tiny, brittle voice. "You're OK, kid," she said to me. "You always have been OK." And then she turned to the rest of the family and she began to laugh. To laugh hysterically. I didn't know how she was able to do it. I hadn't thought she had the strength. But she began to laugh hysterically and to shout, "Fuck you all!"

What? What was she saying? Could this be happening?

"Fuck you all!" she shouted, and her old spirit seemed to be struggling to return. Joy, actual joy, seemed to inhabit her as she shouted again and again, "Fuck you all! The whole family!" And she was crying with laughter and rocking back and forth in her bed.

"Rose! Are you out of your mind?" my mother said. "She's out of her mind," she said to a doctor and a nurse who had heard the commotion from outside in the hall and had popped in to see what was happening.

"Fuck you all!" my aunt shouted.

"It's the disease, doctor," my mother said. "It's gone to her head."

"She don't know what she's saying," my Uncle Bernie said.

"It ain't right," my Aunt Evelyn said. "I never heard such

language in my life."

"FUCK THE WHOLE GODDAMN BUNCH OF YOU!" my Aunt Rose shouted in a great joyful exclamation, and she rocked with laughter under the covers. Her face glowed with frenetic happiness, and she caught my eye and squeezed my hand with her shaking fingers. She was crying with febrile excitement, and she continued to squeeze my hand, and to laugh so loud, so hysterically, all the years of her proud spirit came rushing through the room. "Fuck you *all!*" she shouted. Everyone looked as though they had been hit in the smacker with individual patties of shit. My mother continued to apologize to the doctor. The nurse said, "I think you should go now." My father gathered up his cancelled checks. My Aunt Evelyn ushered us into the hall, saying, "It ain't proper. She's outa her mind."

"It's not her," my mother said, nervously. "It's the disease. It went to her brain."

"That's right, Evelyn," my Uncle Sol said. "Ceil's right. It's the disease. It went to her brain."

My Aunt Rose shook there in her bed, the tears pouring down her face, as she continued to cackle and yell, "*Fuck you all!*" The family drifted and rolled back like a huge wave, receding slowly down the halls and elevator and out the big front doors of the hospital.

Chapter *38*

Late in the summer, Aunt Rose died. I had not seen her again after that last farewell when she had told me I was OK and held my hand. My mother kept the news of her death from me and so I missed her funeral. I was working as a counselor at Camp Merryglade. My mother didn't tell me because I was "too young to deal with death," and she didn't want to burden me with the news.

By the time I finished helping them close up the camp after the kids had left, and I came home, ready to go to college, my aunt was already dead and buried. My Aunt Rose was gone. No more would we hear her giggling as she imitated Mrs. Weiss, my old former babysitter, saying, "Oy, is d-d-dat a D-D-Danny! Is d-d-*dat* a *Danny*!" No more would we hear her falsetto voice as she tried to keep from giggling when she did her imitations of Eleanor Roosevelt saying, "Think of the mountains! I say think of the prairies! This, yes *this* is Americah to me."

No more would we hear her quietly humming, "Prisoner of Love," and, "My Foolish Heart," and, "I'll Never Smile Again," as she shuffled around her dark apartment in her quilted housedress.

My Aunt Rose was gone, and it was time for me to leave as well. It was time to leave The Bronx and to go off on my own, seeking a wider world, a world of larger scope and greater possibilities.

My parents would make this possible.

My mother, who, with the money I spent in going to college, could have furnished her apartment three times over, who could have gone to Hawaii and Bermuda and Europe and all those places she had never seen, my mother, who could have bought *three* mink coats and thereby *demolished* her rival, Muriel Teitner, my mother talked my father into giving me this chance.

And my father, who not only had never traveled, but who didn't even own a goddamn imitation-leather toilet kit, my father who would walk ten blocks before he would pay a penny to park in the street, my father would beg and borrow thousands of dollars, and, for whatever reason, would in fact get me out of The Bronx, and would give me the opportunities an education afforded, the education that he had never been able to obtain. Yes, my mother and my father would sacrifice whatever it took to see that I got a fair chance to make something of myself in life.

As my Uncle Lenny used to say before he was arrested and died in prison, "Go figure baseball!"

EPILOGUE

In the years that followed, my father continued to slave away in his store, making good on his promise to pay for my college education. He finally paid off the debt he had incurred when he bought out his partner. A few years later there was a scandal in New York State involving a bribe allegedly paid to the State Liquor Commissioner. In order to clear his own name, Governor Nelson Rockefeller, who had appointed the Commissioner, blamed the entire affair on the system of liquor licensing in the state. Coming forth as a champion of the consumer, the Governor succeeded in doing away with the fixed pricing in liquor stores and with the limit on the number of liquor licenses issued.

The department stores began to sell liquor at one cent over the wholesale price. Two new liquor stores opened up around the corner from my father's store. My father, who had worked for over twenty years to pay off the equity that the fixed pricing and the monopoly on liquor licenses had given him, was suddenly left with a store that was worth no more than the value of the bottles of liquor on the shelves.

These reforms wiped him out overnight. He continued to run his store for a few more years, working even harder to make a go of it in his new and difficult circumstances, but he never fully recovered from this blow. One day he fell over dead at the cash register in his store. He was fifty-six years old.

My mother collapsed at the funeral. A while later she moved to Miami where she bought a condominium. After a few years she married a man who, although in his seventies, works long hours in a men's clothing store. I just received a photo from them the other day. They were standing in front of their new Lincoln Continental, each wearing yellow slacks and white shirts to match the new car. She was smiling in the photo. I hope she found what she was looking for, because I wish her the best.

My Uncle Bernie and Aunt Bessie live in a condominium complex in Southern California. While my father had been falling into trouble at his store, ironically, my uncle, who had been drunk for years, struck it rich in the sixties when young people began to spend enormous sums of money on rock LP's. At one point, his doctor told him that if he continued to drink his liver would fail and he would die. He has not taken a single drink since that day. He says every liquor store looks like a funeral home to him.

My Uncle Bernie prays a lot now. Whenever one of his friends is sick, my uncle visits him and tells him jokes. Then he goes to pray for him in the synagogue. His friends call him "The Rabbi." He also prays for his son Louie.

My Cousin Louie the mook continued to gamble and to lose money, finally turning to loan sharks as his debts grew. One day, when he was in his mid-twenties, he left the house for work and never returned. No one ever heard from him.

His parents believe that he is alive and perhaps has moved to another state and changed his identity. Yet the fact that after all these years he has never contacted anybody argues against this. My Cousin Herbie believed that Louie grew increasingly ashamed at owing money to so many people and he committed suicide. Yet few people who knew him think he was the type to commit suicide. No body was ever found, which argues against his theory.

In my opinion, the Mafia finally carried through on their threat to take him for a ride and "break his arm" because of outstanding debts to their loan sharks. Knowing Louie the mook, when they tried to rough him up he would have fought back and they would have had to kill him. Virtually everyone who knew him believes Louie was killed by the Mafia.

My Cousin Herbie made it through the Marines, but when he was discharged he began to act erratically and could never hold a steady job. He kept saying he wanted to be a disc jockey. He moved out of

The Bronx, into a small apartment on the Lower East Side in Manhattan, near where his father was born. He continued to come up to his mother's apartment and to bother her and the neighbors. He also began to act aggressively toward me, in spite of the fact that I often gave him food, money, and a place to sleep. After I got married, he even began to send strange, obscene letters to my wife.

One day, on a visit to his mother, he set all the ornamental candles in her apartment on fire. She called the police and had him committed to Rockland State Hospital. After about two years they let him out on probation. He left the state and they never went looking for him. The last I heard, he was taking a lot of speed and living in a cheap hotel in New Orleans on a mental disability pension from the Marine Corps.

As for myself, I don't go back to The Bronx very often. No one I know lives there anymore, and much of The Bronx is in ruins: a violated, bombed-out, enrubbled sad hulk of a city.

I did make it through engineering school, and I became an engineer, but I was looking for something else. In fact, I endured many changes of direction, and I went through perhaps more than my share of periods of despair—despair with myself, my family, my friends, my country, and, at times, with the entire human race, but somehow I was always able to find a source of fresh strength deep inside myself which enabled me to proceed. It wasn't until many years later that I came into conscious knowledge of what had always been ciphered on the scrolls of my cells, in the codes of my genes: I was a descendant of pioneers.

My grandparents. All four of them. Jewish kids who had left everything behind and had dared to sail the great ocean without recourse, to a new land across the world, a life or death gamble on the possibilities of change. They were young people, supported by a ship of desperate dreams, without money, without even that more precious medium of exchange, the common currency of their new land, the English language.

That was the secret which I had always held but which took the better part of half a century to reveal itself to me: I descended from pioneers who had crossed the ocean of no return.

When I realized this, I was forced to recognize that I too was engaged in a long and dangerous voyage from which there was no

187

turning back. I was signed on for a life and death journey into the nuclear age.

My generation did not have to go to sea. On August 6, 1945, the sea came to us.

It was going to be a dangerous trip, but somehow I continued to hope that we could make it through. I hoped we would not let happen to the entire world what we had let happen to The Bronx.

Somehow I knew, if we were brave enough, we could make it through to a land we had not yet been able to imagine.

THE END